Mommy's Home, Princess

An ABDL and MDLG story of a middle girl who needed a Mommy more than she knew, and the perfect Mommy to teach her how to be a good girl

By Tina Moore

Table of Contents

Chapter 1

"Well, well, what do we have here?" Samantha quietly said as she sat down in a café after work, opening up the newspaper. Samantha was a regular at the café and would stop in for a caramel latte after work most days. She worked downtown in a busy office as the HR manager. After being at the company for over ten years, she had become bored with the day to day tasks that awaited her every morning. She took comfort in the fact that at least her job was easy and gave her time to get her nails done during her lunch break or go shopping with her friends. At 45, her figure was beginning to show her age with her hips having gained a few extra kilos over the last year, and her large breasts starting to grow heavy. Yet apart from this, she still looked like a glamour model and never had a hard time finding women to share the night. Her hair shone chestnut and chocolate brown through the window of the café as she looked out the window and sighed. It was Friday, and she had nowhere to be. She thought about heading to the gym, or giving the new girl she was chatting to online a message, taking her phone out just to put it back into her long felt coat.

"Can I get this to go?" She asked as she stood up. The waitress hurriedly put the slice of black forest cake into a paper box and handed it back to Samantha.

"See you Monday," she happily said to Samantha, who smiled politely.

That's a bit tragic. I need to find somewhere else to go. Samantha thought to herself as she pushed the glass door of the café open and walked out onto the street.

She pulled her coat tightly around her body as she felt the crisp bite of the afternoon on her lips. Being the tall woman she was, it wasn't long before she found a quick rhythm and paced quickly, wanting to warm up as the cold air began to settle in for the night. As she turned the corner, she saw a girl that she just knew she would love to take home. The girl was lean, wearing the no-label type of clothes Samantha herself hadn't purchased in over two decades. Her hair was a light blonde, and her green eyes looked up at Samantha as she passed her. Samantha couldn't help but get turned on by the girls' big eyes and sad face, wishing she could have scooped her up and held her tight like a lost little puppy needing love.

Sweet little thing. Samantha thought to herself as she opened her apartment building door and walked inside. She walked across the lobby and pressed the elevator button to her penthouse.

"I should probably take Holly out for a walk actually," Samantha said out loud as she rode the elevator to the top floor. Holly was the black Belgian Sheepdog Samantha had bought two years ago. Samantha had a wood cabin two hours from the city where Holly and her would escape to most weekends so that Holly could run around, but during the week, she had to settle for a walk and run around the off-leash dog park three blocks from the penthouse.

"Come here, darling," Samantha said as she walked through the door. Holly jumped up from sunning herself in the living room and almost knocked Samantha over in delight and excitement.

Walking down to the street, Samantha numbed out the strangers who passed her, wishing that the emptiness in her heart would leave her alone. Samantha and Holly reached the dog park only to find that they were the only people out that afternoon.

"Well, Holly, I guess you have the run of the park," Samantha said, finding a wooden bench and sitting down, her heeled knee-high chocolate brown boots crossed over her thighs. Samantha sighed and watched as Holly sprinted around the park. She closed her eyes and rolled her head back, trying to feel the last of the sun before it went down, only opening her eyes when someone sat down next to her on the bench.

"Hi," came a soft, gentle voice. The sun went

down, and Samantha saw the girl before her shiver, making Samantha lick her bottom lip seductively.

"Hello," Samantha replied, eyeing the young woman more predatorily than she meant to. The black-haired woman with piercing blue eyes made Samantha bite her bottom lip as she turned her head to look away.

Fuck me, Samantha thought, her body instantly tingling. She rolled her eyes at herself, deciding that she needed to get out of there before she was even more tempted to lay the girl down and have her way with her right there on the bench.

"Are you from around here?" The girl asked, her eyes wide and innocent-looking looked up at Samantha's face. Samantha couldn't help but smile down as she looked into the girl's eyes, pausing a moment before replying.

"Yes, but I haven't seen you before. Is that your new puppy?" Samantha replied, tilting her head towards the small golden retriever with the big puppy dog paws trying to keep up with Holly.

"Yep, I got her three months ago. I try to take her out when there are not so many people here because she's so little," she explained.

"I guess I'll be seeing a lot more of you then," Samantha said, the suggestive tone in her voice making the girl giggle.

"Maybe," she replied, looking out toward the dogs. Sensing the girl pull away from her, Samantha extended her hand.

"I'm Samantha," she offered, smirking a one-sided smirk when the girl's smaller hand fit sweetly into her larger one.

"Nelly," the girl replied, a wicked gleam in her eye intriguing Samantha.

"And I'm 26. You know, for when you invite me to have a drink with you," Nelly replied, holding her breath and biting her lower lip, her eyes sparkling with mischief.

"That's very presumptuous of you," Samantha said, holding onto her hand a little longer than necessary. Nelly just shrugged her shoulder, the wind picking up her shiny black hair and floating it in the breeze.

"I'm free tomorrow at 7. I'll meet you here," Nelly replied, getting up to walk away. Samantha quickly got to her feet, enjoying how she towered over Nelly, making her pussy instantly wet. Samantha's older body was soft and curvy, and Nelly's mouth was in perfect alignment with Samantha's large, thick nipples.

"I wouldn't usually take orders from someone so little. But I will see you then," Samantha said, whistling to Holly, who came bolting over to where the two women stood.

"I wouldn't have had to if you had backed yourself," Nelly teased, before clipping her baby, pink leash onto her puppy and walking away.

What the fuck just happened? Samantha thought as she softly chuckled to Holly as they headed in the opposite direction. Holly looked up at her, and Samantha could almost swear she was smiling at her.

Samantha took her time getting ready the next day. She had gone to the salon and gotten her hair freshly blown out, her nails done, and her body massaged.

Even if baby girl stands me up, at least I will look divine, she thought to herself as she laid out multiple outfits on her king-sized bed. She had decided that even though Nelly had made the first move, the bar they would go to was going to be Samantha's choice. She wasn't interested in going to a loud club with dance music and instead had made a reservation at an expensive cocktail lounge which overlooked the glittering lights of the city. There was a particular table which Samantha had requested, knowing that it was secluded and private. She was secretly hoping that Nelly wouldn't be appropriately dressed, making it look like Samantha was her sugar Mommy. She liked it when her girls didn't match with her. She also liked it when they were either under or overdressed. This mostly made them slightly self-conscious and feel vulnerable and made Samantha feel like she was truly protecting them because they would instinctively lean into her and be more open to her affection.

She looked over her-self one last time, running her hands over her voluptuous body, the red satin dress hugging her full-figured curves perfectly. Her silver heels giving her extra height she didn't really need, and her hair, nails, and make-up looking flawless. She sprayed her body with perfume before heading out the door.

Nelly was already waiting at the dog park when Samantha whistled at her, causing her to turn around, and her mouth gape open.

So you fucking should, Samantha thought to herself, seeing the desire in Nelly's eyes. Samantha smirked, her eyes taking all of Nelly in. Her hair was tied and slicked back in a flawless pony-tail, her black leather skirt had a loose white t-shirt tucked in, and her heeled combat boots made her thigh muscles stay flexed. Her silver sequined jacket lay on the bench next to her small red clutch purse.

"Hi sweetheart," Samantha said, pulling Nelly in by her wrist and wrapping her arms around the smaller woman. Nelly held her breath, worried that her knees would give way if she let herself relax into Samantha's cuddly embrace.

"Hi," Nelly replied when Samantha finally let her go and took a step back.

"I think I should go change," Nelly said, her gaze wide and untrained, looking over Samantha's body, not sure where to rest her eyes.

"No, you look lovely. Come on. I've made a reservation at a place I know you'll like," Samantha said, reaching out to take Nelly's hand in hers. Nelly whipped her head around and looked up at Samantha, Samantha seeing this out of the corner of her eye and smiling.

There's my cheeky girl. She thought to herself as she saw the gleam of mischief in Nelly's eyes.

"How do you know what I'll like?!" Nelly teased her playful giggle at the end of her question, making Samantha's heart warm.

"Because, it's the perfection influencer spot," Samantha knowingly said, silencing Nelly.

"I've got nothing for that one," Nelly said, somewhat impressed that Samantha wasn't letting her take the lead.

"I know you don't," Samantha laughed back, pulling Nelly into her as they walked past a rowdy sports bar as a group of men were coming out. Nelly giggled and wrapped her arm around the older woman's body, resting her head onto the side of Samantha's breast as Samantha pulled Nelly closer as they passed the group.

"You know, I can defend myself," Nelly said, pulling away from Samantha as they turned the corner.

"Oh, I am sure you can. But when I'm around, you won't have to," Samantha said, looking Nelly dead in the eye and unnerving her once again.

"Ok," Nelly replied, her first moment of surrender written in her eyes. Samantha loving smiled at Nelly and continued to walk up the street and toward the cocktail lounge.

"Here we are," Samantha said as they reached the door, and a wide-eyed Nelly followed her inside.

They were shown through the lounge and to their table, and Nelly sat down, looking out the window and down on the city, which roared with life outside.

"This is really nice," Nelly said, looking back up and around at the luxurious space. She hadn't noticed Samantha had ordered two cocktails and was taken by surprise when her drink was placed in front of her.

"So, this is going really fast. You're really affectionate," Nelly said, smiling in disbelief that she was sitting across from the beautiful woman.

"We can go slower if you like. I could have taken you to an average restaurant, had an average meal and conversation, but you don't seem average. And yes, I am you didn't seem to mind," Samantha said, taking a sip of her drink and letting her words sink in. Nelly raised her eyebrows in agreement.

"Fair point," Nelly said when she finally replied.

"So, what's your deal, then?" She added, making Samantha laugh.

"My deal?" Samantha questioned playfully.

"Yeah, like, what do you do for work and that sort of thing. Do you always pick up girls at the dog park?" Nelly teased, making Samantha laugh.

"I'm a HR manager, and no I don't, but I think we both know you picked me up baby girl," Samantha said watching how Nelly responded to the pet name, getting turned on when Nelly slightly blushed and swallowed before looking for her drink to take a sip.

"I'm 45, single. I like younger women. I live in an apartment overlooking the city, and I like pretty shiny things," Samantha added, somewhat boring Nelly, who sipped her drink.

"Now tell me something a little less

superficial. Tell me about your first heartbreak," Nelly said, excited to see Samantha's reaction.

"You are such a cheeky girl," Samantha said, signaling the waitress and ordering a selection of tapas before looking at Nelly with the dominating glare she would have saved for a much later occasion.

"Tell me about yours first," Samantha ordered more than asked. Nelly thought about the statement before smirking and shaking her head no.

"I kinda asked you first," Nelly replied, causing Samantha to smile on the inside, although continuing to stare Nelly down. Samantha kicked off her heels under the table and placed her freshly pedicured feet on either side of Nelly's chair, taking her by surprise.

"You want to play that game, do you?" Samantha said, her voice becoming serious. She sensually moved her feet over Nelly's thighs and parted them. Nelly complied willingly but kept her eyes on Samantha, not sure what to make of the women sitting across from her. Samantha kept her feet on Nelly's chair, forcing her thighs apart as she raised an eyebrow at Nelly before gently stroking her over her panties. Nelly gasped and sat up straight, pulling away from Samantha, but Samantha's legs were long enough that Nelly couldn't actually get away from Samantha's touch. Nelly clenched her jaw while looking at Samantha with wide, surprised eyes before looking around the room. Biting her bottom lip, she rolled her hips forward, pushing herself against Samantha, who enjoyed watching Nelly crave more of her touch.

"Ok, I'll go first," Nelly said, a flush of pink covering her cheeks as she stumbled on her words.

"I was 19. Her name was Daniela. She was way too old to be fooling around with a teenager, and I was way too young to be trying to gain the affection of a woman. She was German. Her accent was so incredibly sexy. I really liked her, but I didn't know what the hell I was doing, and she thought I was only using her for a ride home. It took years to get over her. She was everything I thought I wanted in a partner. She was tall, dominant, affectionate, caring, stylish, and so sophisticated. But I was a kid and way too immature to be able to be with anyone, and it didn't get very far. We tried to have sex. It was so bad! She came in only wearing a towel wrapped around her hips one time. Her abs were breathtaking. She was in the army when I spent time with her. It was one of those tragic moments in life that I look back on and cringe. Like how could she have even entertained the idea of fucking with me?! I can't imagine being with a 19year old now, let alone when I will one day be her age. I kinda just threw myself at her. It was a complete trauma bond and response, which I've since corrected, sort of. But I'm glad now that it didn't work out, coz I wouldn't have had the incredible life I've had or be sitting here with you if it hadn't turned to shit for me at least. She probs never gave me a second thought, but it took me years to get over her," Nelly explained, taking Samantha aback by how open and forthcoming

Nelly was about her first heartbreak.

"Wow," was all Samantha said as she took in the words Nelly had just poured out onto the table.

"Trauma bond and response?" Samantha asked, making Nelly giggle.

"Another time, yeah?" Nelly asked, her eyes telling Samantha that this wasn't something to press on.

"Sure," Samantha said, sipping her drink.

"So, you like older women then? I don't have the body of the woman you just mentioned," Samantha said, annoyed at herself for wanting validation. She knew she was attractive, but she hadn't seen her abs in years and was surprised that Nelly made her question her appearance.

"Yeah I do, I like how they make me feel, I don't know why I just always have. My tastes are diverse. You have things she didn't. Don't worry, Mama, you're good," Nelly said, winking at Samantha playfully.

That's the only problem with all this

normalization of kink. Girls be calling you Mommy without actually knowing what they are saying, Samantha, said to herself, hoping that Nelly wasn't just being friendly but actually knew what she was referring to.

Chapter 2

Samantha and Nelly had stayed in the bar until closing, walking out onto the street in the early hours of the morning.

"I haven't been out this late in ages!" Nelly exclaimed, stumbling into the back of Samantha as she walked.

"Come here, angel," Samantha said, turning around and holding Nelly as her knees buckled.

"Oh my god, how embarrassing," Nelly giggled, snuggling into the older woman as they waited for a taxi. Samantha whistled one down, unknowingly turning Nelly on and helped her into the backseat.

"I don't want you to go," Nelly said, reaching for Samantha.

"Make sure she gets home safely," Samantha said to the driver before taking Nelly's hands in hers and kissing them.

"I'll see you soon, princess," Samantha said before pulling away from her and closing the door. They had exchanged numbers, and Samantha sent her a message almost immediately.

I have had the best time in a long time, thank you, darling, the message read before Nelly smiled and closed her eyes.

Nelly woke in the morning and turned over in bed before she opened her eyes. She loved that split second between sleep and being awake. She could feel the stillness of her mind, and it made her smile for the moment of pure peace. She heard her phone go off and looked to see she had a missed call from Wendy.

"Fuck!" Nelly moaned out in frustration. Wendy was Nelly's most recent ex, and although they had broken up several times, she was like the party drug Nelly couldn't seem to leave alone. Opening the voice message, she knew that it wouldn't be good and winced, ready to hear the attack.

"I need to come over to get a few of my things. We are done this time. When are you free?" Came the voice down the phone, and Nelly bit her lip looking at the time.

Like, now would be fine, Nelly replied via text message, seeing Wendy reply almost immediately.

Good, see you in an hour, came her answer, and Nelly groaned and threw her phone into her bed. Quickly, she got out of bed and raced around her small apartment, collecting Wendy's things, she didn't want this to take any longer than necessary. She and Wendy had met at a party years ago and had hit it off straight away. Wendy had felt like a safe space for Nelly, and they had moved in together shortly after becoming official. The problem was, Wendy liked to drink and became aggressive with Nelly. She had hit Nelly on more than one occasion, and it had taken Nelly all her youthful courage to leave Wendy, just to fall back into her life, time and time after that. Wendy always promised that she would get help, see somebody, sort it out, and it was good for a while, months at a time, just so long that Nelly would let her guard down and then Wendy would unravel all over again, each time becoming worse than the last. Nelly hoped that Wendy would just take her stuff and go, she didn't want a scene, not today.

"Hi," Nelly said as she opened the door to Wendy, standing on the other side.

"Hey," Wendy replied, looking better than Nelly had wished she did.

"Can I come in, hun?" Wendy asked, dipping her head to meet Nelly's eyes.

"Don't call me that," Nelly softly said as Wendy pushed past her and into the apartment.

"Everything is in that box. You can just take it and go," Nelly said, trying to maintain some kind of control over the situation.

"Or, I could grab a cup of coffee, and you can tell me how you have been?" Wendy offered. Nelly just shook her head. She couldn't believe how innocent and kind and gentle Wendy sounded. It was a far cry from the violent rage she dished out last time Nelly was in her presence.

"I just need you to go," Nelly replied, walking back over to the door and opening it. Wendy eyed her angrily, not happy about being told no. She got up from the sofa, picked up the box, and sauntered toward Nelly, placing the box on her hip and reaching out, taking Nelly's jaw in her hand before Nelly could stop her.

"You'll never find anyone who loves you more than me, remember that this is what you wanted," Wendy cruelly said, aggressively letting Nelly's jaw go, her tight grip leaving red marks on Nelly's cheeks and tears in her eyes as she slammed the door shut. Nelly slid down the back of the door and cried into her knees as she held them to her chest and tried to calm herself. Reaching into her shorts pocket, she pulled out her phone and replied to Samantha's message.

Same here, I'd love to do it again sometime, typed Nelly before putting it back into her pocket and getting up, deciding that she needed a hot shower.

Nelly pulled her thin jacket tighter around her waist as she waited for Samantha outside her tall office building. She had half a mind to cancel their plans as she was looked up and down by the countless suits who passed her in the lobby.

"Hi sweetheart, sorry I'm a bit late. My last meeting ran overtime," Samantha said as she reached out to embrace Nelly, pausing when she saw the bruises on each side of Nelly's cheeks. She hadn't done as good a job at covering them up as she had thought, but Samantha didn't mention it and held onto her firmly.

"Ready to go?" Samantha eagerly asked, Nelly just silently nodding and trying to look confident. Samantha sensed the girl's distant behavior and held out her hand, her eyes warm and loving, and Nelly gave a half-smile and held her hand as they left the building.

Walking down the street, Samantha slowed her walk to match Nelly's shorter stride and affectionately rubbed Nelly's hand with her thumb. Her heartbeat racing as Nelly reached out to cuddle her arm as they walked. Stopping once they reached the pier, Samantha sat down on a bench and pulled Nelly close into her.

"Do you want to tell me about it, sweetheart?" Samantha whispered into Nelly's ear as her hand ran through Nelly's hair. Nelly thought for a moment before shaking her head, only snuggling further into Samantha, who kissed her forehead and held her as they watched the waves crash onto the sand. Samantha looked over the sand and watched as the seagulls danced in the sky, wondering what was going on in Nelly's mind that could take her so far away. The afternoon sun warmed her hair, and as Samantha sighed and ran her fingers through her hair, Nelly reached out and touched her thigh.

"I am trying to do something I don't usually do. I'm trying to wait, but you have no idea how sexy you are," she said, looking up at Samantha and getting lost in her eyes.

"Yeah, baby girl, you can't fuck the pain away. Not with me anyway," Samantha replied, reaching out and stroking Nelly's cheek.

"So, um. There is this ex I have, and she's a bit violent. She did this," Nelly said, showing Samantha the bruises on her face. Samantha frowned and felt her heart hurt with how Nelly's eyes swelled with tears.

"Shh, it's ok, sweetheart, come here," Samantha said, feeling more connected to this woman than she could have predicted.

"I just feel like such a loser. Like I thought I was stronger than this, you know?" Nelly asked, wondering if Samantha would up and run, wondering if this was all just too much leftover drama to start something new. Samantha was wondering the same thing, hoping that she wasn't getting into another project that would just up and leave when she had put her back together.

"Look," Samantha said, pulling away from Nelly slightly to turn and look at her.

"I think that maybe you need to take some

time to sort this out for yourself. I don't mind helping you through it, but I don't want to be a bandaid for your broken heart," Samantha explained. Nelly just nodded her head.

"Well, she came and picked up the last of her stuff this morning so it is well and truly over," Nelly said, half laughing when Samantha tilted her head and looked at her unconvinced.

"Yeah, but these tears are fresh, honey. So it's not as over as you want it to be, not yet," Samantha said, reminding herself that Nelly might not even be the type of girl she needed.

There's a big difference between a damsel in distress and a baby girl, Samantha, reminded herself. Standing up and stretching before holding her hand out to Nelly, who all but jumped into her arms.

"Dinner?" Nelly suggested. Samantha had to think about it, but Nelly's warm body snuggling into hers got the better of her and she opened her coat to keep her extra warm as they began to walk back into town.

Chapter 3

"You look really nice," Nelly almost whispered as Samantha sat down by the window seat in an Italian restaurant. This was the sixth time they had met up over two weeks, but Samantha felt like she had known Nelly for months. She smiled, seeing the blush cover Nelly's cheeks and watching as she sat down.

"I thought you might like it," Samantha replied, looking down at her thick navy cable knit pullover. It made her breasts look even bigger than they were, which is why she had worn it. She subtly smiled to herself before looking back up at Nelly.

"I could just dive right into you," she said, refusing to hold back any longer. Nelly bit her bottom lip, her eyes sparkling.

"Well, we are in a public place, that would be highly inappropriate," she teased, causing

Samantha to raise her eyebrows.

"What I would do to you would definitely cause a few heads to turn," Samantha replied, not missing a beat. Nelly could feel herself getting turned on and looked away to try and regain composure. Nelly wasn't sure how to move their relationship along. They had gone on coffee dates, been to the movies, and on a picnic, but every time Samantha got too close, Nelly would push her away. Samantha knew this too, and so they both sat in silence while they waited for their order to be ready.

"Do you want to come to mine after this?" Samantha asked suddenly. Nelly thought for a moment, a mix of lust and fear in her eyes.

"For, maybe hot chocolate?" Nelly said, trying to hint that she didn't think sex was a good idea tonight. Samantha nodded her head, understanding the younger woman's meaning, making Nelly smile.

"Yeah, ok then," Nelly said, leaning back and having her pizza placed down in front of her by the waitress.

"I should have just assumed," Nelly laughed as Samantha pressed the top button on the elevator.

"Well, it's just that the view is far nicer at the top," Samantha replied, leaning back against the elevator mirror and placing her hands on her hips, eyeing Nelly.

"Don't look at me like that," Nelly giggled, turning around and ignoring Samantha.

"Like what?" Samantha whispered into Nelly's ear as she wrapped her arms around Nelly's waist and pulled her body back into hers. Nelly felt her pussy contract immediately, and her breath quicken.

This is going to be harder than I thought, she thought to herself as she felt Samantha's hands gently rub her sides.

"We are here," Samantha said, having seen that Nelly had closed her eyes to try and keep herself from turning around in Samantha's arms.

Opening her eyes, Nelly saw the luxury penthouse suite in all its glory and was speechless.

"So, you aren't coming to mine anytime soon!" Nelly exclaimed as she followed Samantha into the kitchen, making her laugh.

"Drink?" Samantha asked Nelly, who just nodded plainly as her eyes took in the space. Samantha poured two glasses of chilled wine and led Nelly over to the sofa. Sitting down, Nelly sunk into the soft fabric and let out a contented sigh.

"This isn't hot chocolate," Nelly cheekily pointed out. Samantha ran her hand through her hair before resting her head on the back of the sofa.

"No, but there's plenty of time for that," she replied.

"You are certainly comfortable here," Nelly said, feeling mildly out of her comfort zone. Seeing this, Samantha leaned forward and took the glass from Nelly's hand.

"Let's see if we can make you just as comfortable," Samantha said, taking Nelly's hand

and pulling her into her lap.

"Don't fight me, honey, let me love on you a little," Samantha said as she felt Nelly's body stay rigid and somewhat afraid. Samantha stroked Nelly's hair until she felt her body relax and snuggle into hers. Wrapping her arms around Nelly, Samantha fantasied about having this as a part of their bedtime routine and Nelly in cute little socks and dressed in a onesie. Her thoughts got interrupted by Nelly shifting and laying in the perfect position to nurse, making Samantha's heartbeat race.

"I think I am too tired to go home," Nelly said as she closed her eyes and turned into Samantha, who held her tight. Samantha bent her head and kissed Nelly's cheek as Nelly brought her hands up and placed them at her chest.

"Do you want to stay the night with me, sweetheart?" Samantha asked, brushing the hair out of Nelly's eyes as she nodded yes.

"Hold on then, honey, I'll take you to my room," Samantha said as she stood up, Nelly in her arms much to her surprise.

"I didn't think you were that strong," Nelly said, her eyes wide in disbelief.

"There are a few things you are yet to learn about me," Samantha replied before walking into her room, pulling back the sheets and placing Nelly in bed. Samantha crawled into bed next to her and held her gently, biting her bottom lip when Nelly put her thumb in her mouth in her sleep.

Nelly woke to the sound of silence. She turned her head to see that Samantha was lying on the other side of the bed, both their clothes still on from the night before. Getting up, Nelly tiptoed out of the room and into the living room. Holly was on the floor but was undistracted as she played with a toy. Nelly decided to try and find the bathroom and began walking through the apartment. She passed the huge artworks hanging elegantly on the wall and the media room with the big green pool table in the middle. She walked out onto a balcony, which led to a spa and sauna. Looking over the balcony rail, she watched as the world buzzed under her feet and sighed, surprised that she was in this place and feeling like an imposter. Nelly walked back into the apartment through a different door, finding herself in the type of room she had only seen in porn videos. Raising her eyebrows, she reached out to touch the black satin drapes and let her eyes roam, slightly overcome with what she was seeing. The thick black carpet felt soft underfoot, the large bed in the middle of the room looked inviting, but the flogging cross in the corner made Nelly shudder. The toy box in the corner of the room made her tilt head to the side in confusion. She began to lift her foot to step further into the room when she heard Samantha clearing her throat behind her, making her spin around and gasp in surprise.

"You need to ask to go in there, sweetie," Samantha lovingly explained. Nelly realized her mouth was opened and shut it quickly, trying to brush what she had seen off like it was nothing.

"Oh, sorry, I kinda got lost," she said,

sidestepping Samantha and beginning to walk away, turning back slightly to see Samantha following behind her.

Nelly walked back inside and went to sit down on the living room sofa and collected her things in the type of rush that made Samantha uneasy.

"I better get going," Nelly said, unsure of how to be around Samantha now that she had seen her sex room.

"If that's what you want," Samantha lazily said, making herself a coffee. Nelly stopped packing her stuff into her leather handbag and turned to face Samantha.

"So when I asked you what your deal was, you didn't think to tell me that you were, are, some sort of sadistic dominatrix?" Nelly said, rather accusingly. Samantha tried to suppress a smirk before coming back over to Nelly, her red bra showing through her white satin dressing gown.

"Why would I have said that I was a sadistic dominatrix?" Samantha innocently asked as she sipped her coffee. Nelly just scoffed and stuffed her jacket into her bag.

"Um, hello, because you have a fucking sex dungeon in your house!" Nelly replied, pointing in the direction of the room with her whole hand and waiting for an answer.

"I have that room, yep, but I am no sadist. I'm a Mommy, but I still like to punish a girl," Samantha said, placing her hand on Nelly's thigh and affectionately squeezing it.

"The fuck does you being a Mum have to do with it?" Nelly asked in frustration, not understanding what Samantha was talking about.

"Um. So, no. I'm a Mommy Dom, darling. If I am going to have a sub, she has to identify as either a middle or a little. Not all the time, I am no charity, but like, a little more than 50% of the time," Samantha said, getting lost in how much of a baby girl she truly enjoyed having. Nelly just put her head in her hands and sighed.

"I've got to go," she suddenly said, getting up, only stopping as Samantha grabbed her wrist.

"Can we talk about this, baby? This is not

how I wanted you to find out," Samantha asked, letting Nelly's wrist go as she pulled away.

"Not right now," Nelly said as she walked over to the elevator and impatiently waited for the doors to open. Walking toward hers, Nelly turned around, more fear in her eyes than Samantha would have liked to see.

"Don't come over," Nelly hesitantly asked, causing Samantha to stop in her tracks.

"You don't need to be afraid of me. You can say no without me forcing you, and you can get in that elevator without me locking you out," Samantha said as the doors opened, and Nelly hesitated, taking one step in and letting Samantha's words sink in.

"I'll text you later," Nelly said as she got into the elevator, the doors closing slowly, Samantha's face disappearing and the decent causing Nelly to exhale like she had been holding her breath for years.

Chapter 4

Nelly didn't text. She didn't call, and she didn't message over social media. After a week of silence, Samantha was beginning to wonder how much longer Nelly needed, and if there was any point in reaching out herself.

Maybe I should just forget about her. She thought to herself as she entered her usual café after work.

"Hey, I haven't seen you around lately," the waitress said as she walked over to where Samantha was sitting. She was young, roughly the same age as Nelly, and Samantha wondered if the longing in her voice was directed towards her.

"Well, I've been a little busy. Have you missed me?" Samantha playfully teased, watching as the waitress tried to get her blushing cheeks under control.

"Um, so, the usual," Tammy, the waitress

asked, pulling her hair to one side.

"No. Surprise me with something new," Samantha replied, enjoying the fluster she was causing the girl. Tammy left in a hurry, making Samantha chuckle to herself as she opened her paper just to close it again.

"Hi," Nelly said. Nelly had sat down just as Samantha opened her newspaper, causing Samantha's eyes to widen.

"Hi?" Samantha questioned, raising her eyebrows at Nelly.

"Yeah," Nelly said, unsure of why Samantha seemed guarded. Samantha looked at Nelly, her 'come save me' stare, giving off more energy than usual.

"Ok. How have you been?" Samantha asked, folding her newspaper down and surrendering to the situation.

"Fine. Sorry I didn't message or whatever. I just needed to get my head around the fact that you're like...you know," Nelly stammered. Samantha thought for a moment.

"Baby. If you can't handle this, that is totally ok. Don't stress about it," she said, enjoying Nelly's indignant look when told she couldn't handle the situation.

"Yeah, that's what I'm trying to tell you. That's why I wanted to do this in person. I think maybe I could, like it," Nelly said, annoyed that their dynamic wasn't as affectionate and loving as before.

"I don't want to have to force it on you, and I don't know if you'd be into it or just trying to please me," Samantha explained, making Nelly pout, her eyes filling with water. Samantha stood up and moved seats, sitting next to Nelly and bringing her in for a cuddle before pulling back to wipe her tears.

"Shh, it's ok, honey," Samantha said, not being able to help herself from smiling at Nelly.

"But what if I wanted to try?" Nelly said, looking up at Samantha and giving her the biggest puppy dog eyes.

"Tell me what you think you want to try?"

Samantha asked, seriously considering Nelly's offer.

"I want to be with you, like, be your girlfriend and then like with the sex stuff, try doing the stuff you like. I've just never done anything like this before, it's always been pretty basic," Nelly explained, half convincing Samantha that this could work. The waitress came back with a slice of Honey cake and a vanilla latte, giving Samantha a sad smile just as she walked away.

You need to stop flirting with everyone. Now you need to give the girl a generous tip, so she doesn't think you are an asshole, Samantha thought to herself as she passed Nelly the latte.

"Have a sip," Samantha said to Nelly, who obeyed her without question.

"It's pretty good, here," Nelly said before handing the glass to Samantha.

"I don't think diapers are for me," Nelly suddenly said, causing Samantha to choke on the warm liquid and start to laugh.

"So, you want to talk about this here, right

now?" Samantha asked, her perfect eyebrows raised as she put the glass on the table.

"Well, yeah. We could whisper," Nelly said, mischievous eyes sparkling, making Samantha just roll hers.

"So I've done a bit of exploring online, and I think I'd sort of be more a middle than a baby coz like I don't really have any desire to play with baby toys and stuff," Nelly said reaching for the Honey cake, getting her hand swatted away.

"What does a relationship like that even look like," Nelly said as Samantha leaned back in her chair and watched Nelly's excited face.

"Depends. I have had relationships that were completely caregiver centered and ones that have had no element of kink at all, but the later isn't what I am looking for," Samantha explained.

"So, what are you looking for?" Nelly asked, taking a sip of the latte once more. Nelly wondered if she would look as glamorous as Samantha when she was her age. Her wavy hair that came down just under her breasts, her long eyelashes, and puffy lips. The stare that seemed to intimidate Nelly and turn her on at the same time made Nelly smirk.

"What happens in 25years when I am not exactly young anymore?" Nelly asked, making Samantha laugh.

"Let's just get through this conversation first, honey," Samantha laughed, taking a bite of her cake.

"It's like everything darling, it'll take time to figure out our rhythm, but I want to try with you too," Samantha said, letting her heart get the better of her. Nelly looked at the woman she believed was way out of her league, and her surprised eyes made Samantha laugh.

"Come on, little girl," she said, standing up, leaving a $10 tip and holding out her hand to Nelly, who took it eagerly as they left the café.

Nelly waited on Samantha's bed, wondering what was taking so long. Samantha had been in her room-sized wardrobe for the last ten minutes, and

Nelly wondered what on earth could be taking so long when Samantha said she was only changing into something more comfortable.

"Sorry, honey," Samantha said as she came out of the double-doored room, making Nelly roll her eyes. Samantha wore her hair down, her pink sweatpants were tight on her ass, and the white singlet under her grey zipped up sport hoodie made Nelly blush.

"Well, now, I am over-dressed!" Nelly playfully complained, making Samantha smile.

"Shall we then?" Samantha said, taking Nelly's hand and twirling her around before she led her through the apartment and to the playroom. Feeling Nelly pull back on her hand, Samantha turned to her, coming over to kiss her on the top of her head.

"We aren't fucking tonight, baby girl, don't worry," Samantha said as Nelly cautiously looked into the room that was primarily designed for sex. Nelly looked up at Samantha, her puppy dog eyes aching to be able to trust the Amazonian goddess who stood in front of her.

"Ok," Nelly said, biting her lip and following Samantha into the room. Samantha sat Nelly down on the bed and went over to the free-standing cupboard by the far wall of the room and opened both doors.

"Want to come and find something you can relax in?" Samantha asked, as Nelly slowly walked over to where she was standing, cuddling into Samantha almost involuntarily as she looked.

"These are cute," Nelly softly said, slightly regaining her confidence as she flicked through the clothes. Taking out a pair of thigh-high pink stripy socks, Nelly smiled and kept looking, stopping when she saw a short pair of white shorts and a matching t-shirt with a kitten on the front. Looking back at Samantha, Nelly shyly smiled and bit her bottom lip before Samantha took the items and led Nelly back to the bed.

"Can I help you put them on, honey?" Samantha asked, sitting down on the bed and having Nelly standing in front of her, between her thighs, nodding shyly.

"Ok, come here," Samantha said as she reached out and took the front of Nelly's jeans in her hand and jerked her forward, making Nelly fall onto her lap, her hands on Samantha's thighs making her smirk. Samantha expertly unbuttoned Nelly's jeans and wriggled them off her hips, gently caressing Nelly's thighs, making her giggle somewhat nervously.

"It's ok, sweetheart. Mommy's got you," Samantha said, Nelly, exhaling loudly, realizing she had been holding her breath. Samantha wondered how long it would take for Nelly to drop her guard and let the little girl within her to come out and feel safe, deciding that time would tell as she finished dressing her.

"There," Samantha said as she leaned back on her elbows, Nelly standing in front of her. Nelly looked down and ran her hands over the shirt and looked back, and smiled at Samantha.

"What now?" She innocently asked, Samantha pushing the thoughts of ripping the clothes off of Nelly to the side.

"We could snuggle on the couch, watch a movie?" Samantha suggested, seeing the wicked grin of Nelly's come back across her face.

"Only if I can pick," Nelly said, giving Samantha a cheeky look before turning and bolting out of the room. Samantha laughed as she followed Nelly to the living room and sat on the sofa as she watched Nelly look for how to turn on the tv.

"Looking for this?" Samantha teased as she held her phone up, Nelly tilting her head to the side in confusion.

"I control everything in this house with my phone," Samantha said, feeling smug as Nelly looked to the side and walked to the couch, snuggling into Samantha.

"So, it looks like I'll be picking the movie," Samantha whispered as she wrapped her arm around Nelly as she flicked through the possible options. Settling on a mild action rom-com about two spies, Samantha heard Nelly's tummy rumble.

"Hungry, baby girl?" Samantha asked,

hoping that what was going to come next wouldn't cause Nelly to run away. Nelly nodded her head and watched as Samantha began to massage her breasts sensually.

"Um, what are you doing?" Nelly asked, already knowing the answer.

"Well, you could have some milk," Samantha suggested, taking Nelly aback slightly, causing her mouth to gape open, as Samantha confirmed what she had thought.

"You don't have to, you also don't have to try and stay within a particular 'age,' you can just enjoy what you enjoy, and maybe you'll enjoy this?" Samantha explained. Nelly began to blush as she fought with herself to give in to what she wanted to do but hating herself for feeling weird about it.

"I, um," Nelly stammered, watching Samantha unzip her hoodie slowly and lift her singlet.

"If you hate it, forget it. But come and try honey. Can Mommy take the lead?" Samantha asked, seeing Nelly struggle with her desires and her shame as she silently nodded, happy to have Samantha take control. Samantha lay Nelly over her lap and held her tightly, stroking her cheek with her thumb as her other hand positioned her nipple into Nelly's mouth. Squeezing her breast, Samantha watched as Nelly's eyes grew wide as she tasted her milk for the first time. Nelly could feel her heart wildly beating before something came over her, and she closed her eyes and relaxed into Samantha's arms and moaned contently.

"There you go, little one, let Mommy look after you," Samantha said as she patted Nelly's tummy gently as she watched the girl suckle. Nelly felt her head rush with a feeling she hadn't felt before. Something between ultimate safety and complete calmness, a set of feelings she wasn't used to feeling, her eyes beginning to fill with tears, and the pain she carried with her was soothed.

"You're safe, honey, Mommy's got you,"

Samantha whispered as she watched Nelly's blue eyes turn navy as she let the tears fall down her cheeks. Samantha held her, only stopping when Nelly tried to sit up and pulled Samantha's singlet back down.

"Are you full, sweetheart?" Samantha asked, kissing Nelly's furrowed forehead, Nelly only nodding as she snuggled into Samantha and watched the rest of the movie in silence.

Chapter 5

"Mommy," Nelly whispered the next morning. Samantha had let Nelly stay over, and she smiled as she saw Nelly's face close to hers with the morning sun coming in behind her.

"Good morning, sugar," Samantha sleepily replied, rolling over to check the time. Nelly jumped up on the bed and waited for Samantha to turn back around

"I made breakfast," Nelly said proudly, causing Samantha to look at her suspiciously.

"You made breakfast? I distinctively remember you telling me you couldn't cook," Samantha teased, grabbing Nelly and pulling her back under the covers and wrapping her up in her arms and legs. Nelly giggled as she struggled to get away, causing Samantha to get turned on as she rubbed her clit and nipples in her attempt to escape.

"Ok, ok, I bought it," Nelly giggled as she surrendered to Samantha, who had taken to gently patting her bottom.

"That's what I thought," Samantha said, letting Nelly turn around in her arms and lay on top of her, Nelly, snuggling into her breasts.

"But I put it on plates," came Nelly's muffled response as Samantha pulled her singlet down and pressed Nelly's mouth onto her nipple, holding her willing head in position as she continued to pat Nelly's ass, smirking when she felt Nelly begin to grind on her thigh.

"That's what I expect, little darling," Samantha said, gripping onto Nelly firmer as she felt Nelly's thigh pressing into her wet mound.

"Oh, little one. You aren't ready for me just yet," Samantha teased as she playfully spanked Nelly's ass before pulling her head back by her ponytail, milk dripping from her lips and landing back on Samantha's breast.

"Come on, let me see what you have gotten up to," Samantha said, Nelly's whingeing eyes making her smirk.

Nelly had bought croissants, breakfast juices, and scrambled eggs and had set it out elegantly on the dining room table, Samantha nodding her head, impressed with the girl's efforts.

"Nice job, honey," Samantha said as she sat down and began to eat.

"I wanted to say thank you," Nelly said, sipping her juice. Samantha frowned, looking at Nelly with curiosity.

For what?" Samantha asked. Nelly laughed and looked at her, thinking she was joking.

"I've never been with somebody who is so, gentle and kind and lovely. I feel like you're more than I deserve," Nelly confessed. Samantha scoffed and shook her head.

"Oh, honey," she replied, reaching out and stroking Nelly's cheek affectionately, before pushing her chair out and patting her lap. Nelly stood and moved to sit on Samantha's lap, cuddling her as she finished breakfast, enjoying how open with her body Samantha was and how much affection she so freely gave.

Nelly practically skipped into work on Monday morning, delighted with life for the first time she could remember. Samantha felt the same as she sat down in her big office chair, she smiled up at the ceiling and sighed in contented bliss. The phone rang, breaking Samantha's happy train of thought and answering it, she had to clear her throat to sound like the ballbusting manager her colleagues knew her to be. Nelly's job was a little less formal, as she pulled on her work uniform, she straightened her tie and rolled her eyes.

Time to sell some holidays, she thought to herself, noting the vast difference between who she was last Friday and who she was today. Nelly worked as a travel agent and was grateful she could keep her phone on her as she worked, sending Samantha dirty messages throughout the day.

You need to stop, I am about to go into a meeting, and my panties are already soaked you wicked little thing, Samantha messaged as she left her phone in her briefcase and headed into the meeting. Nelly just smiled as she too put her phone away, excited to see Samantha in a few hours. They had decided to meet up for dinner at a new Japanese restaurant that had been getting rave reviews online, and Nelly thought about how she was going to seduce Samantha that night.

"So, how was your day?" Samantha asked as Nelly sat down at the restaurant 5mins late. She had missed her train and had to catch a later one. She was grateful that Samantha didn't seem to care.

"Yeah, fine. The usual. Somebody booked a holiday in South Africa, which looks really exciting actually. They have booked one of those tours around an animal park where they are the ones in the cage so the animals can roam free. I really like that concept. Wild animals shouldn't be locked in cages," Nelly said, Samantha, enjoying the conversation and excitement in Nelly's voice.

"I agree. It is quite cruel," Samantha replied before ordering. They talked through the night, laughing and throwing back shots until they were asked to leave because the restaurant was closing for the night.

"Oh, sorry, come on, baby," Samantha said, getting up and walking to the counter to pay.

"I'll be outside," Nelly said, squeezing Samantha's hand affectionately as she pushed the door open and walked into the cold night air. Breathing in, Nelly smiled a genuine smile, feeling like all the stars had finally aligned.

"There you are," Samantha's voice cut through the air, Nelly turning around and half jumping into her arms, Samantha opening her coat and wrapping it around Nelly.

"Come on, Mommy, let's go home," Nelly whispered as she kissed Samantha on the cheek.

"I want to see what's under that dress," she quickly added, blushing at her remark.

"Do you now?" Samantha replied, winking at Nelly, admiring how wide-eyed and innocent she looked. A taxi pulled up, and they quickly got in, eager to get home.

"You're not going to need this anymore," Samantha said, taking a baby wipe from her handbag and sensually wiping Nelly's crimson lipstick off her lips. Nelly was grateful the driver got all the green lights on the way to Samantha's apartment and practically jumped out of the car when he pulled up at her building. They walked in silence, through the lobby, both imagining what was about to unfold.

"Can I kiss you?" Nelly said the moment the elevator doors closed. Samantha eyed her hungrily.

"I would be offended if you didn't," she replied, reaching out and pulling Nelly into her, embracing her fully and almost leaving Nelly breathless. Nelly's lips met Samantha's, and as they passionately kissed, Samantha tenderly pawed over Nelly, finally able to touch her where she had wanted. The elevator doors opened, and Nelly took a step back, just to find Samantha step forward and envelop her once more, making her giggle.

"Wait. I need to catch my breath," Nelly laughed, worried her asthma would begin to play up if she continued.

"I can't have you needing to rush to the emergency room," Samantha playfully said, slowly taking off her coat and letting I fall on the marble floor. Nelly watched as Samantha began to unzip the back of her dress and stood before Nelly in just her lingerie and heels.

"Fuck, I'm lucky," Nelly said in her girlish voice, making Samantha swoon. She pushed Nelly back down on the bed and kicked off her heels before lying next to her.

"Take off your shoes," Samantha instructed, watching as Nelly obeyed her command.

"And your jeans," Samantha continued, watching as Nelly wriggled to her get jeans off. Nelly went to take her panties off, stopping when Samantha placed her hand on top of hers.

"Not yet, your shirt," Samantha said,

redirecting Nelly. She unbuttoned her silk blouse and lay in her lingerie next to Samantha, shivering as the air conditioning cooled her skin.

"Get under, baby girl. Mommy can't have you getting cold, can I?" Samantha said, making Nelly smile. Samantha turned on a slow melodied soundtrack and began running her hands over Nelly, kissing her gently as she snaked her way down and then back up Nelly's body.

"I usually wouldn't be so nervous. You just make me so nervous," Nelly whispered, unable to summon that cheeky and playful girl she was sometimes.

"That's ok honey, can I take the lead?" Samantha replied, Nelly, nodding her head and gasping as Samantha quickly turned her around and sat behind her. Samantha let her hand roam over Nelly's tummy, snaking them down until she slipped them under her panties, making Nelly push her head back against Samantha's large breasts and moan.

"You are such a wet little thing," Samantha

said, her words fanning the fire that had built inside of Nelly for weeks now.

"Spread your legs for Mommy," Samantha instructed, Nelly following her commands. Nelly bit her bottom lip and moved her hips as she softly moaned while Samantha stroked her clit.

"You're already so swollen for me. This is what you wanted?" Samantha said as she slipped a finger into Nelly, who raised up on her hands, surprised by the intrusion. Samantha just wrapped her other arm around Nelly's waist and pulled her back down, making her take the finger inside of her as she wiggled it.

"Shh, just relax, little bunny. Mommy is going to treat you real nice," Samantha said, feeling Nelly's muscles begin to contract, sliding in another finger and working her clit at the same time.

"Mommy," Nelly whispered in a long breath, closing her eyes and slightly rolling into Samantha as she was fucked. Samantha pulled her bra down and pushed Nelly's mouth onto her nipple, smiling as Nelly instinctively began to suckle using both hands to lift Samantha's breast to her lips. Samantha pumped her fingers harder and faster inside of Nelly as she suckled, feeling her own juices begin to drip onto her panties. Nelly moaned into Samantha, only adding to her arousal, and as Nelly bucked her hips aggressively against Samantha's hand, she came hard. Nelly looked up at Samantha, and her eyes rolled to the back of her head as she closed her eyes and melted into Samantha's embrace. Samantha smiled, gently took her hand from the younger girl's pussy, and licked her fingers clean.

"Sweet little honey," she said, pulling down her panties but waiting for Nelly to come down from her orgasm. Samantha stroked her body, enveloping her as she made sleepy noises while she snuggled.

"I thought that might be the case," Nelly said as she opened her eyes again after feeling inside Samantha's panties. Samantha enjoyed keeping a neatly trimmed, thick bush, which Nelly explored as she touched Samantha's body. Nelly slid her fingers between Samantha's thick pussy lips, and just as she was about to enter, Samantha pulled her hand away, laughing when she saw the look of confusion on Nelly's face.

"I want it on your mouth, little one. Can Mommy sit on your pretty little face?" Samantha asked. Nelly nodded and pulled her long hair to one side. Samantha moved over Nelly's face and pulled her panties to the side, lowering gently onto Nelly's lips. Nelly stuck her tongue out and made Samantha shudder as she was licked slowly.

"That's it, honey," Samantha moaned, subtly rocking her hips and grinding her pussy against Nelly's tongue.

"Suck Mommy's clit, baby," Samantha instructed, pleasure clear in her voice. Nelly obeyed, moving between teasing her pussy with her tongue and sucking her clit, gently at first, but then with more passion as Samantha's juices began to drip onto Nelly's tongue.

"Oh baby," Samantha moaned, grinding

hard on Nelly's face as she came. Nelly wriggled under Samantha's thighs, making her smile as she took her time to get off the younger woman.

"Let's get you cleaned up, sweetness," Samantha said, wiping her cum off Nelly's lips before kissing her gently. Samantha noticed the tears forming just behind Nelly's eyes and paused.

"Did I hurt you, baby?" Samantha asked, concern in her voice. Nelly just shook her head and tried to wipe the tears away, getting up and quickly walking to the bathroom. Samantha followed her, stopping Nelly from shutting the door on her.

"Hey, come on, talk to me," Samantha said, sitting on the edge of the bath, watching as Nelly paced back and forth.

"I don't know what to say. I just feel all churned up inside, and I shouldn't because like you are awesome," Nelly blurted out, looking at Samantha fearfully, worried she would push her away.

"Tell me about sex with your ex," Samantha

said, taking Nelly by surprise. She looked at Samantha, who just looked at her knowingly and waited.

"It was rough, really physical and aggressive, I guess," Nelly thoughtfully replied, looking at Samantha with confusion.

"And tell me about the sex we just had," Samantha instructed. Nelly came to sit next to her, resting her head on Samantha's shoulder.

"It wasn't like that. It was soft and gentle and passionate," Nelly said as she remembered how safe Samantha had made her feel.

"So, do you think that you might not know how to handle feeling safe and vulnerable at the same time, and that's why you're a bit freaked out?" Samantha said, leaning back to turn on the bath.

"Maybe," Nelly said, letting Samantha put her into the bath as the water warmed up. Samantha raised an eyebrow at Nelly, making her laugh and shake her head.

"You must think I'm so lame that I can't

even figure myself out," Nelly said as Samantha poured in relaxation gel into the water before joining her.

"No, honey, I don't think you are lame. I think you just need Mommy's love, and that's exactly what you are going to get," Samantha replied, pulling Nelly into her arms and gently rocking her as she calmed down.

Chapter 6

Samantha drove Nelly home in the early hours of the morning, tucked her up in bed, and waited until she was asleep before she left, kissing her forehead before she closed her apartment door.

Oh, this girl, Samantha thought to herself as she smiled on the drive back to her apartment. Samantha had a bad track record of girls, never being able to keep a relationship for longer than a year or so, and she desperately wanted to keep Nelly. She couldn't wait until Friday when she would be able to hold Nelly once more, and Samantha drove to work for the next four days, craving to have her baby girl back in her arms.

"Sorry I'm late, meetings," Samantha said, rushing into the bar, kissing Nelly full on the lips as she sat down. Nelly just giggled from behind her glass of whiskey and rolled her eyes.

"I think that might be something I have to get used too, huh?" Nelly asked as Samantha looked at her apologetically.

"Maybe?" Samantha replied, hoping that it wouldn't be a big deal.

"Well, if you keep coming with gifts, I think I can handle that," Nelly teased as she looked at the design shopping bags Samantha had walked in with.

"Funny you mention that. It was exactly what I was trying to do," Samantha said, winking at Nelly and passing her a bag.

"If you don't like them, we can go and get you something else. I saw these on my lunch break and thought how sweet they might look on you," Samantha explained as Nelly took out the earring box and opened it, her eyes going wide as she opened the box and saw the pink diamond studs in a rose gold setting. Nelly looked up in shock, making Samantha laugh as she ordered a drink.

"Can I help you put them in?" Samantha asked as Nelly nodded, smiling as she took out her silver hoops.

"I have never had something like this before," Nelly said as she opened the camera on her phone and looked at her gift.

"I just couldn't go passed them," Samantha replied, sipping her cocktail and admiring Nelly.

"Thank you, Mommy," Nelly whispered in Samantha's ear as she affectionately hugged her before sitting back down and tucking her hair on one side behind her ear.

"So, it's the weekend. I kinda have a few ideas," Nelly said, taking the print out of her bag the word document she had constructed of all the adult baby things she liked the look of, taking Samantha by surprise.

"Really?" She questioned, somewhat impressed that Nelly had taken some initiative.

"Like, maybe not all at once, but yeah," Nelly said as she got up to stand next to Samantha, who wrapped her arm around Nelly's waist as they looked at the ideas together.

"I can work with this. Come on, baby girl,"

Samantha said, feeling her nipples begin to leak in anticipation. Nelly grabbed her backpack and coat and followed Samantha out of the bar.

"So, not as big as you thought you were, huh?" Samantha questioned as Nelly reached for the paci that Samantha held just out of her reach. Nelly was dressed in a short pair of denim shorts and a cropped white t-shirt, her abs on clear display, and a pink bow headband in her hair.

"Mommy," Nelly whined as she reached for the paci, Samantha giving in to her cute puppy dog eyes and pushing it into her mouth.

"Can we do that lego set together, Mommy?" Nelly asked, taking a bite of the Salmon Samantha had made for dinner.

"Yep, a little later. Mommy wants to watch the news first. Come and cuddle with me," Samatha said. Nelly got up from the table and took her plate over to the couch and sat on the floor between Samantha's thighs as Samantha played with her hair.

"This is really scary," Nelly said as they watched the segment about terrorists. Nelly got up and walked back to the kitchen and put her plate in the dishwasher before coming back and snuggling into Samantha. Nelly distracted herself by playing with Samantha's breasts, enjoying making her nipples hard and lazily nursing. Samantha absent-mindedly rocked Nelly and patted her thigh until the news ended. Laughing, Samantha looked down at Nelly, who had fallen asleep with her nipple in her mouth. Slightly moving, Nelly's eyes opened sleepily, and Samantha rolled her onto her back and pulled a fluffy blanket around Nelly, tucking it in as she went to shower and change into her pajamas.

"Mommy," Samantha heard from her bedroom, smiling when she saw Nelly at the door.

"Yes, little one?" Samantha asked as she pulled her soft robe around her and tightened it. Nelly reached her arms out to her, and Samantha wondered how she had gotten so lucky.

"Can we do lego now?" Nelly asked as

Samatha looked at her expectantly.

"I think you are forgetting a very important word, young lady," Samantha said, seeing the mischief in Nelly's eyes.

"I don't think I am," Nelly replied, causing Samantha to laugh.

"Well now, I guess Mommy has to remind her little girl to use manners," Samantha said, taking Nelly's wrist in her hand and pulling her over her lap. Nelly was no match for Samantha, and she secured her hands behind her back and her legs down with one thigh.

"Where do you think you are going, little girl? Mommy has you now," Samantha teased, as she began to run her fingernails over Nelly's bare skin, giving her goosebumps. Samantha and Nelly had spoken at length about the type of punishments that they would both be comfortable with, and Samantha was excited to be able to test out one on Nelly.

"Oh, I'm not going to spank you, honey," Samantha said, causing Nelly to stop moving, her mind racing at what could come next. Samantha pulled Nelly's pants down before she spat into her hand and placed it against Nelly's pussy, spreading her lips quickly and rubbing her clit forcefully.

"Mommy is going to force orgasm after orgasm on you, sugar. You're going to be wrecked once I am done with you, and all you are going to be able to do is moan the word please until I am satisfied," Samantha said, using a stern voice Nelly hadn't heard before. Nelly hadn't thought the Samantha would try this punishment out of something she thought was only mild disobedience, but as Samantha rubbed her clit, she moved her hips in time to Samantha's touch.

"What are you doing, baby girl. Mommy hasn't said you could move," Samantha said, causing Nelly to moan as she tried to stay still, her pussy contracting with desire, her thighs flexing. Samantha fucked Nelly agonizingly slow, making Nelly groan in frustration for fifteen minutes before letting her cum, only to continue her onslaught, refusing to give her any recovery time.

"What do you need to say to make Mommy happy, baby girl?" Samantha asked.

"Please, Mommy," Nelly breathlessly said, dragging out the words as another orgasm washed over her body.

"That's right. From now until I tell you, they are the only words allowed to escape that pretty little mouth," Samantha said as she placed her hand in Nelly's hair, grabbing a fist full and pulling her head back as she fucked the girl lying over her lap.

"Please, Mommy," Nelly begged, involuntarily bucking her hips violently as she came again only to be continually fucked.

"Good girl," Samantha replied, leaving her clit alone and sticking two fingers into Nelly's wet pussy and hearing her gasp as she was filled. Samantha pumped her fingers in and out of Nelly until her forearm ached, causing the girl to rest limply over her thighs as cum poured from her pussy.

"Please, Mommy," Nelly wearily moaned,

almost calling red just as Samantha pulled out of her and turned her around, so she was looking up at Samantha and getting squished into her breasts.

"Don't make Mommy have to teach you that lesson again," Samantha warned as she pinched Nelly's nipples through her shirt until she flinched.

"Yes, Mommy," Nelly said, her eyes glazed over and her body exhausted.

"Good girl. Let's get you cleaned up," Samantha said, lifting Nelly in her arms and taking her to the bathroom to shower.

"And because you have behaved like such a baby not knowing how to say please, you can wear a diaper tonight to help you remember," Samantha said as she lay Nelly down on her bed.

"But I'm not that little, Mommy," Nelly whined as wriggled and fought Samantha, losing as Samantha successfully diapered her and pulled on her pajamas.

"I don't know about that, you look pretty little right about now," Samantha said, picking Nelly up and carrying her to the living room and put her down near the table where her lego box was and watched as she pouted.

"Don't complain about it, or I'll make you wet it too," Samantha warned, making Nelly's eyes go wide and look away.

"That's better. Now, can Mommy help you make this?" Samantha asked, pulling Nelly into her lap and brushing her hair from her eyes.

"Yes, please, Mommy," Nelly replied, the mischief in her voice, not escaping Samantha as she helped her open the box.

Chapter 7

"Baby girl, Mommy is home," Samantha called from the door of their new house. Samantha and Nelly had moved into an apartment just outside of the city together. It wasn't the luxury penthouse suite Samantha was used to, but it was more beautiful than any place Nelly had ever lived. Holly and Sasha, Nelly's golden retriever puppy who wasn't such a puppy anymore, got along, which made them all living together simple and easy.

"Hey, Mommy. I'm in here," Nelly yelled from the kitchen. Samantha rolled her eyes, wondering where 'in here' was as she hung up her bag on the wall hook and began uncuffing her cufflinks.

"Oh baby," Samantha said as she walked into the kitchen to find that Nelly had been busy, from the looks of things, for hours.

"I wanted to make you dinner, and dessert," she said proudly. Samantha rolled her sleeves up and looked around the kitchen.

"And you left Mommy with the washing up?" Samantha teased, grabbing Nelly and kissing her passionately before holding her in her arms as she looked over to the dining room table and saw the delicious spread Nelly had prepared.

"So we have carrot soup with thick-cut bread to start, roast duck and seasonal vegetables as main and for dessert," Nelly said, pausing and leaning over to the fridge to show Samantha the chocolate cake she had made.

"Mudcake!" she said proudly. Samantha kissed her cheek.

"You are so wonderful," she said as she walked over to the table and sat down.

"How was your day?" Nelly asked as they began to eat. Samantha rolled her eyes.

"Everyone there is a complete idiot, and I hate them all. But apart from that, it was fine. What did you get up too?" Samantha replied, noticing that Nelly had already fed the dogs.

"How long have you been home?" She added, wondering how Nelly could have had time to pull this off in the thirty-minute time difference between Nelly getting home and Samantha finishing work.

"Yeah, so, I kinda wanted to talk to you about that. I've changed jobs. It just wasn't working for me anymore, and I wanted something that is going to make me feel happy and not caged in," Nelly began to explain. Samantha wondered why Nelly hadn't talked to her about her feelings, but she stayed quiet. In the six months they had known each other, Samantha had grown to learn that Nelly liked to make a move before she announced it.

"I saw that the music store down the road from my bus stop was looking for admin staff. So I went in there yesterday afternoon and asked a few questions, and they said they would be happy to take me on and yeah. I signed the contract this morning. I went into work to give them my two weeks' notice, but the boss was so mad she made me take my holidays instead, so I was home by like ten and decided that I would make you this great dinner," Nelly said, making Samantha smile.

"Well, here's to you, my love," Samantha said, raising her glass of wine and toasting to Nelly.

"You're not mad?" Nelly asked. Samantha frowned.

"Why would I be mad? This is your life, baby girl. You can make any decision you want in it. Mommy is just here to help you when you need me, but you didn't need me for this. You put your big girl pants on, and I am so proud of you. I am especially proud that you cooked! I might have to get you in that kitchen a little more regularly," Samantha laughed.

"But I think dessert will have to wait, honey. I am so full, and I want to fix up your nails tonight. I can't have my pretty girl getting around town looking unloved, and that chipped color is driving me crazy. Mommy is going to have a shower, you clean up as much as you can, and I'll do your nails once I'm out, alright?" Samantha said, getting up from the table and walking over to Nelly, kissing her on her forehead before disappearing into the bathroom.

There was something about Samantha that made Nelly want to please her. It was unlike anything she had ever experienced in the past, and she smiled to herself when she finished putting away the dishes just as Samantha came out of the bathroom.

"Baby, I didn't expect you to get all of it done. Oh, you are such a good girl for Mommy," Samantha said as she fawned over Nelly, loving the way Nelly snuggled between her breasts.

"I was thinking. Maybe I could get black, please, Mommy?" Nelly asked as Samantha, and her sat down in the nook they had turned into a nail salon set-up. The nail salon where Samantha used to get her nails done had closed down, and she had been unable to find a studio she liked, so she had gone out and bought everything she needed to do their nails at home. She had even made Nelly watch hours upon hours of nail tutorials to make sure that she could do nails as well.

"Really? I was thinking more a sweet baby pink?" Samantha teased. Nelly just rolled her eyes and giggled.

"Mommy, I'm too big for baby pink," Nelly said, reaching for the black. Samantha took a moment to look at Nelly in her grungy little outfit and smiled.

"Well, you are allowed to be too big for baby pink, but you aren't allowed to get too big that you don't want these anymore," Samantha said, shaking her breasts in Nelly's face making her giggle before she began to do Nelly's nails.

"Do you think that we could go to the park on the weekend? I heard there is a really nice market that's held every Sunday. Maybe we could pick up some yummy food and have a picnic?" Nelly suggested as she watched Samantha.

"Yeah, we could. I was hoping to unpack a

few more boxes, though, so it just depends on how much we get done, honey," Samantha replied as she concentrated.

"Ok," Nelly replied, just as Samantha finished up.

"There, all done, baby girl. Now, Mommy wants a little quiet time tonight. Do you want to do your sticker by number book or go online for a while?" Samantha asked. She and Nelly had decided that they needed to restrict Nelly's screen time after Samantha had woken up to Nelly still being online at 3 am when they had gone to bed at 10 pm the night before.

"Online!" Nelly half squealed, wrapping her arms around Samantha, who held her lovingly before letting her go.

"Alright, see you in a little while," Samantha said as Nelly bounded off into her own little space in the apartment. There was an outdoor space that came with their apartment, and Nelly had transformed it into something like a fairy garden. There were strung up fairy lights and bean bags and comfy blankets, and she settled in with a hot chocolate for a few hours of mind-numbing online entertainment. She had often wondered what Samantha was up to during her quiet times, even having snuck in a few times to look at her without her knowing. But she would always just do the same thing, sit in her chair by the fire and sip Scotch. It wasn't that she was a big drinker, but every now and then, she just wanted to be left alone. Nelly had been grateful when Samantha had told her that it wasn't personal; it was just something she needed to do to unwind from a day sometimes. Nelly had thought that maybe she was texting someone else, but Samantha had put that fear to rest by taking her lock off her phone and allowing Nelly to check her phone and emails whenever she felt the need. When Samantha had told her friends that Nelly checks her phone and emails, they had been concerned, saying how she should be allowed to have her privacy, but Samantha just laughed. What was so private that she was doing? Getting emails from the juice bar where she had a loyalty card telling her she can have a free birthday juice? Samantha had explained that Nelly needed more reassurance that she wasn't going to get hurt and that she was more than happy to give it to her.

"What are you up too, baby doll?" Samantha said as she sauntered outside to were Nelly was sitting. Nelly looked up just as Samantha came to sit down next to her and wrapped a blanket around herself.

"This is sobering. It is freezing out here!" Samantha said the alcohol she had felt pumping through her veins only moments ago by the nice warm fire slowly disappearing into memory.

"I haven't noticed," Nelly replied, looking at her fingers and noticing how blue they were.

"And that is why Mommy doesn't let you go online whenever you want," Samantha said, taking Nelly's phone and putting it in her pocket.

"How's everyone?" Samantha asked. Nelly didn't talk about her family very much, and her friends were the people she worked with.

"Fine. Nobody is doing anything particularly interesting. Although some people from my old job are thinking of going out tomorrow night and they've invited me. I said I'd see if we had any plans first," Nelly said, amusing Samantha.

"Imagine if you told them the truth, that you had to check with Mommy to see if you had been a good enough girl to go out," Samantha teased, making Nelly laugh.

"Yeah, baby girl, go. Do you need me to drop you off or pick you up?" Samantha asked, Nelly just shaking her head no.

"Ok then, well, I'll be here if you change your mind, ok, princess," Samantha added before standing back up and taking Nelly by the hand as they went inside.

Chapter 8

"I don't know if I want to let you out of the house after all," Samantha said as she looked at Nelly walk into the living room. Samantha had decided to order take out Chinese for dinner and put her chopsticks down as she saw Nelly stand in from of her.

"You think I'm pretty, Mommy," Nelly asked, teasing Samantha by sitting down on her lap and wrapping her arms around Samantha's neck.

"Yes, I do," Samantha said, feeling her pussy tighten with desire. Samantha had bought Nelly a pair of pink heels, and she had teamed them with a sparkly silver dress that stopped just under her ass and dropped low between her breasts. Her hair had been straightened and pulled back with a sparkly silver clip, and her make up was natural yet alluring.

"I've got a little bit of time before I need to go, Mommy," Nelly whispered in Samantha's ear, running her hands through her hair and kissing her affectionately as she felt Samantha reposition her. Her hand falling in between Nelly's thighs, brushed her pussy, and her other hand supported her neck, and Nelly tilted her head back.

"Gets you every time, little one. Not such a big girl now, are you? You're Mommy's little plaything," Samantha said, pulling Nelly's thong to the side and sliding her fingers up and down the girl's wet slit.

"Please, Mommy," Nelly begged, igniting the fire in Samantha's eyes. She continued to stroke the girl, who wriggled on her lap, desperate to be given release.

"You do know how to be a good girl for, Mommy, don't you?" Samantha asked as she pushed her two fingers into Nelly, rubbing her g-spot and making her begin to moan with her eyes closed.

"Tell Mommy, you like it," Samantha said as

she felt Nelly dangerously close to orgasm. Nelly bit her bottom lip and began to play with her tits, moaning and moving her body on Samantha's lap.

"I like it, Mommy. I want it so bad, please, Mommy," Nelly begged.

"No, you're not there yet. Mommy is going to make you wait a little longer. I know your body now, baby girl, you can't trick, Mommy," Samantha teased, quickening her thrusts just enough to drive Nelly wild but not enough to give her release.

"Please, Mommy, let me cum, please," Nelly yelled as a banging came from the door. Samantha placed her hand over the girl's mouth as she took her over the edge, making her squirt and cover Samantha's hand in her pussy juices. The banging continued much to Samantha's amusement.

"Just a minute," Samantha yelled out, happy when the banging stopped as she lifted up her girl and led her to the bathroom.

"Mommy," Nelly said in her groggy, afterglow making Samantha giggle.

"Baby girl, you've got a big night ahead of

you, you can't fall asleep now," Samantha said as she cleaned Nelly up all the while Nelly only wanting to snuggle into Samantha's huge breasts.

"But Mommy," Nelly murmured, Samantha finally giving in and placing her nipple in Nelly's mouth.

"You can nurse when you bring your no doubt drunken ass home to Mommy, ok, baby girl?" Samantha said, fixing Nelly's hair before she took her nipple out of her mouth and pulled her singlet back up.

"I don't even want to go now," Nelly half whined as she walked to the door.

"You will once you get there. Have fun, little one. Remember to text Mommy if it's all too much," Samantha said as she playfully spanked Nelly's ass as she walked out of the door.

Samantha was right. Nelly did get in the mood the moment she had her first drink. The music was loud, her friends and her look glorious, and the dance floor had just enough people to make it fun, but not enough to make it crowded. As Nelly dance, she felt how the music took her away to a place she hadn't been in a long time, and she smiled to herself, thinking about how great her life had become.

It was a few hours off dawn when she reached into her purse to take out her phone. Her friends wanted to stay out later than she had thought they would, and after an hour of trying to convince one of them to come back with her so they could leave together, she had lucked out. Taking her phone out, she hoped that Samantha wouldn't be mad to get woken up.

"Hey," Nelly slurred, realizing just as she was going to say, Mommy, that she was in a public place.

"I was wondering when I would get this call," Samantha sleepily replied, somewhat glad Nelly had called.

"Yeah, so um, I thought I'd be home by now, but they don't want to come home, but I kinda really do, but I don't want to go by myself," Nelly began to ramble, getting cut off by Samantha.

"Send me your location and then stay there. Mommy is coming to get you, little girl," Samantha said, getting out of bed and grabbing a hoodie as she made her way to the door.

"You're the best," Nelly replied, before hanging up and sending Samantha her location.

"Oh, I know," Samantha said to herself as she whistled for the dogs to follow her.

"Nelly?" A familiar voice asked as Nelly opened her eyes and swayed against a brick wall.

"Oh fuck off," Nelly whispered to herself as Wendy's reflection was in her face as she waited for Samantha.

"Sweetheart, are you ok?" Wendy asked as she looked at Nelly. Nelly began to walk away from her, only to have her grab her upper arm and grip it firmly.

"Where do you think you're going?" Wendy asked, holding Nelly firmly in place.

"Let me go," Nelly said as she tried to pull

away.

"Cute dress," Wendy said, letting Nelly's arm go. Nelly knew that Samantha would be there any moment, and she also knew that she had sent her location to Samantha. However, in her drunken state, she hadn't thought of the possibility of ringing Samantha and telling her what was going on and to meet her somewhere else.

"I heard you don't work at the travel agents anymore," Wendy said, standing next to Nelly, who had her arms crossed over her chest.

"What do you want?!" Nelly yelled, turning to face Wendy. Wendy got off the wall and placed an arm on either side of Nelly, pressed her body against hers, and pinned her there.

"I want you," Wendy said before kissing Nelly passionately, just as Samantha pulled up to see. Nelly bit Wendy's lip, causing her to pull away and reach out of hit her, just as Samantha grabbed her arm, which was in the air.

"I think you better get the fuck out of here," Samantha said to Wendy, who looked angry and confused.

"So, this is who you replaced me with?! Really, I am way hotter than her!" Wendy yelled at Nelly, who sort comfort in Samantha's arms.

"She always ruins everything," Nelly murmured against Samantha, who led her back to the car.

"She's not hotter than you either, Mommy," Nelly said, the fear in her eyes that she would be rejected, not something Samantha had seen for many months all but broke her heart.

"I know she's not, sugar," Samantha said, winking at Nelly and locking the door before walking back to Wendy.

"If you ever come near her again," Samantha began to say before Wendy cut her off.

"You'll what?" Wendy replied. It was true that Wendy was younger and leaner than Samantha, her blonde hair shining in the moonlight.

"I'll fucking finish what I'm about to start," Samantha said as she dropped her fist into

Wendy's cheek before she turned and walked back to the car.

"She won't bother you anymore, honey bun," Samantha said to Nelly as she drove them home.

"Apart from the end, did you have a good night? Your photos are cute," Samantha said calmly as Nelly clung onto her arm.

"Yeah, it was good. She kissed me, you know. Like I'll understand if you want to break up or something," Nelly said, looking up at Samantha with her sad puppy dog eyes.

"Baby, she didn't kiss you, she assaulted you. There is a big difference," Samantha replied, easing Nelly's mind that she would be left heartbroken.

"And no, Mommy doesn't want to break up with you or something, ok? So just get that thought right out of your head," Samantha said to Nelly, kissing her forehead.

"Don't you think you'll get in trouble for punching her?" Nelly asked as they pulled into their car space. Samantha smiled, there were a few things Nelly still didn't know about her, and one of those things was that her family were the type that really shouldn't be messed with.

"No, I think it'll be ok. I don't think she wants to have anything more to do with us," Samantha replied, walking Nelly into the house and getting her a glass of water.

"Shower and bed, Mommy?" Nelly asked sleepily.

"Come on, lovely girl," Samantha said, picking Nelly up as she began to fall asleep and took her into the bathroom. Samantha helped Nelly get undressed and quickly washed and blow-dried her hair before dressing her in a dino onesie and tucking her up in bed.

"I don't think my tummy can handle the feel of any more liquid, Mommy," Nelly said with her eyes closed when she felt Samantha's nipple pressing against her lip.

"Then don't suckle, but it's going in your mouth, honey. Close your eyes now, go to sleep, baby," Samantha said lovingly as Nelly obeyed her like the good girl Samantha had trained her to become.

Chapter 9

A knock came at the door the next morning, earlier than Samantha would have cared for.

"Shh, Mommy's got it," Samantha said as Nelly opened her eyes and blinked sleepily. Samantha got dressed in her best as the knocking became louder, causing Nelly to become curious.

"Mommy, I can get the door if you want?" Nelly asked as she saw Samantha put on her best coat and heels.

"Baby. You know the box that I told you never to open. If I ring you, I need you to open it and find the piece of paper with the name Joe on it and the phone number. I need you to ring that number and tell them, 'Samantha needs your help,' and then hang up. Don't wait for a response, don't say any pleasantries, alright?" Samantha said, causing Nelly no end of confusion. Samantha kissed Nelly and ran her fingers through her hair as she sighed and walked to the door, opening it to see that it wasn't who she thought it was at all. Samantha had assumed that Wendy had called the police and that they had come to charge her with assault. But it was just a girl scout wondering if she wanted to buy any cookies. Samantha laughed and handed the girl a ten-dollar bill before closing the door.

"You need to talk," Nelly said from behind the door, taking Samantha by surprise.

"That was some badass hustler shit you just said to me. Who is Joe? What the fuck is going on, Samantha?" Nelly said, causing Samantha to stop in her tracks and look at Nelly the way she hated being looked at. It meant she was going to be punished.

"Nelly. I am going to warn you one time," Samantha replied, somewhat understanding that Nelly had the right to have her questions answered. Nelly sighed, trying to figure out how to asked her questions and still be within the agreed-upon rules of their relationship.

"Mommy, I'm scared. All that stuff you just told me, it sounded like something from a gangster movie," Nelly said, sitting on the bed and watching Samantha undress.

"Well. My family, they know some good lawyers, can we keep it at that, honey? I don't have much to do with them for a reason, and I want to keep you out of their world," Samantha replied, causing Nelly to all but lose her shit in excitement. She got up and ran to the kitchen, took a notepad and pen from the bench, and ran back into the bedroom where Samantha was lying naked in bed under the covers.

Is your family in the mob?! Nelly wrote down in her scribbliest writing and passed it to Samantha. Samantha rolled her eyes and pulled Nelly under the covers with her.

What mob? Samantha wrote back before putting her hand over Nelly's mouth as she opened it to speak. Samantha looked Nelly dead in the eye until she calmed down.

"And that is all we are ever going to talk

about it," Samantha said with a tone which told Nelly more than she needed to know.

"Ok, Mommy," Nelly replied, settling back into bed.

"That's right," Samantha said more to herself than to Nelly, who was already dreaming in Samantha's arms.

Samantha and Nelly fell into a predictable routine of 9-5 working hours, afternoon sport, and Thursday night shopping trips. They took the dogs on mountain hikes on the weekends, and Samantha began to introduce Nelly to her friends over Sunday brunches by the river. Life was easy, it was calm, it was happy, and for the first time in forever, Nelly wasn't trying to fight it. She embraced the glamorous lifestyle that she and Samantha were creating and loved every moment of it.

"Mommy's home, princess," Samantha called from the front door. It was Thursday, and Nelly was excited because there was a new pair of shoes she had been looking forward to buying all week.

"I'm just getting dressed, Mommy," Nelly called from the bedroom. Samantha kicked off her heels and grabbed a beer from the fridge before walking into the bedroom to find Nelly struggling with the zip at the back of her dress.

"Can I help?" Samantha asked, putting her beer down and zipping up Nelly's dress.

"Thanks, Mommy," Nelly said, kissing her affectionately. Turning around and smiling at Samantha, Nelly looked down at the dress she had bought last week.

"Yeah you're cute, and don't you know it," Samantha said as she eyed Nelly.

"I was hoping we could go to the mall a little earlier tonight, Mommy. There's this pair of sneakers I am really looking forward to buying," Nelly said, fixing the clip in her hair.

"Oh, about that. A friend of mine from college is in town and was wondering if we could meet up tonight for drinks? I know we sort of have a plan of what we do, but how about, if it's the only thing we are getting tonight, we get them on the way?" Samantha asked, watching as Nelly thought.

"Yeah, ok. Is what I'm wearing, ok?" She asked. Samantha's friends were always model beautiful with stories of jet setting lifestyles, and for some reason, no matter how friendly they were, Nelly always felt left out. Like she was watching a movie, that she was just a spectator to the conversation.

"You always look so gorgeous, baby girl, what you are wearing is fine," Samantha said before walking into the bathroom to get ready.

"Don't be nervous, she's really lovely," Samantha whispered to Nelly as they approached the bar.

"I'm not nervous," Nelly snapped back, proving Samantha's point.

"Mmmhmm," Samantha replied, before greeting the other woman. She was tall, red-haired with fair skin and green eyes that shone when they landed on Nelly.

"You must be Nelly, Samantha has told me so many wonderful things about you," the woman gushed.

"Nelly, this is Amanda, Amanda, Nelly," Samantha said, sitting down and signaling to the waitress.

"Let's get tequila, for old times sake," Samantha said, ordering three shots and three beers as chasers. Nelly smiled despite herself. She didn't really want to like Amanda, but she was so kind and gentle, taking Nelly's hand and sitting down next to her, almost ignoring Samantha, who just sipped her beer and relaxed.

"So Sammy tells me you two met at a dog park? And that you picked her up!?" Amanda asked, the surprise evident in her voice.

"Sammy," Nelly laughed. She rarely even called Samantha, Samantha, so to hear her with a nickname made her laugh.

"Yeah, I bet you are just used to calling her Mommy," Amanda said, Nelly, freezing instantly and going red.

"Oh, it's alright, hun. I'm a Mommy too. I know how it works," Amanda said, trying to reassure Nelly, but her guard was going back up, and both Samantha and Amanda could see it.

"Come here, baby," Samantha said, knowing that Nelly needed to be closer to her than to Amanda.

"Shy?" Amanda asked as Samantha wrapped her arm around Nelly.

"She gets a little wary of new people. Some people have mistreated her," Samantha said, kissing Nelly's forehead. She passed Nelly her phone and smiled when she snuggled up to her as Nelly began playing games online.

"Cute, though," Amanda replied, Samantha just smiling before she directed the conversation in a different direction.

The night dragged on with Nelly jumping in and out of the conversation, Samantha giving her money to go and buy a burger from another place in town, and Amanda slowly gaining Nelly's trust.

Towards the end of the evening, Amanda suggested that they have chocolate cake, and it was Nelly's pleading eyes that won Samantha over in the end.

"How long are you in town for?" Nelly asked as they shared the slice of cake.

"Three nights. I'm a flight attendant, so I never stay in the same place for too long. I like it, but it means that my home life is always a bit of a mess," Amanda confessed, looking at Samantha.

"Yeah, but you could have from all over the world and just keep them on a rotation," Nelly cheekily suggested, coping a look of Samantha and making Amanda laugh.

"You're trouble," she playfully said, making Nelly giggle.

"I must admit, I have done that a few times, but I am more ready to settle down now. I am jealous of you Sammy, you've got such a sweet, little girl, here," Amanda said, feeding Nelly the last bite of cake.

"And doesn't she know it," Samantha added,

reaching out to thumb away the chocolate sauce from Nelly's bottom lip.

"Where are you staying? Do you want to hang out at ours?" Samantha said as she noticed the wait staff beginning to tidy the bar for closing.

"I can't tonight. But if you are free tomorrow night? We could start with drinks at yours?" Amanda suggested, Nelly, nodding her head before Samantha had even replied.

"I think that's a yes," Samantha laughed as they got up to leave.

"You're a tease, do you know that? Samantha said to Nelly on the way home. Nelly was busy looking at her new sneakers in their box and looked up at Samantha, not having heard what she said.

"Huh?" Nelly replied. Samantha looked down on her confused face and beamed.

"I said you're a little tease. Don't play games with Amanda, she will think you are trying to seduce her, and she'll always take the bait,"

Samantha said as Nelly placed her hand on her thigh.

"Just like you did, Mommy?" Nelly teased, making Samantha laugh but roll her eyes.

"We haven't even spoken about adding people to the mix. Is that something you would be down for?" Samantha asked, Nelly's face becoming serious.

"I don't know, that seems like a lot. I think I would be down for it if you are. Maybe not sex, but defs some play with dynamic stuff," Nelly replied. Samantha hadn't realized that she was hoping that Nelly would say no sex and smiled to herself.

"I'm glad you said that. I don't feel comfortable sharing you sexually, but I can handle the power play stuff too. I'll let Amanda know that you might be in little space when she comes over tomorrow if that's cool?" Samantha asked. Nelly thought about it, before nodding.

"Maybe she can help me with my sticker by number picture?!" Nelly exclaimed as Samantha continued to drive them both home.

Chapter 10

"Why are you so stressed out, Mommy?" Nelly asked as she sat on the bed, watching Samantha get increasingly flustered.

"Because I hate everything that I own," Samantha said as she pulled off the shirt she had on and threw it angrily on the bed. Nelly wondered why she was so worried, she'd never seen Samantha loose control before, and it made her nervous. She got up and slowly made her way over to Samantha, looking at her before going to the cupboard and taking out a pair of tailored black jeans, matching heels, and a thin cashmere top, passing it shyly to Samantha.

"What about this?" Nelly asked, making Samantha calm down and see how she had unnerved Nelly.

"Thank you, baby," Samantha replied, pulling Nelly into her arms and kissing the top of her head, letting Nelly cuddle before she let her go.

"Amanda is used to me having a particular lifestyle and," Samantha began making Nelly blush.

"And this isn't good enough for her?" Nelly said, trying to figure out what Samantha was going to say.

"I'm not ashamed or embarrassed about our place, honey. It's just that I don't want Amanda to look down at me. I have known her for decades, and she can be a bit of a show-off," Samantha tried to explain. Nelly just nodded her head. She could see that Amanda liked to have the world's attention.

"Well, if she is mean, Mommy, I'll just bite her," Nelly said, playfully biting into Samantha's arm.

"You will not!" Samantha replied, spanking Nelly's ass and making her run out of the room, giggling down the hall.

A knock came twenty minutes later from the door, and Nelly got up to get it.

"Let me," Samantha replied, eyeing Nelly to sit back down where she had been working on her artwork. Samantha usually let Nelly wear what her heart desired, but tonight Samantha had chosen her outfit. She and Nelly had fussed over the bow Samantha wanted in her hair. Nelly wanted to wear her skinny jeans and a metallic loose fitting singlet with her black faux fur and leather jacket, but Samantha had other ideas. So Nelly had ended up in her skinny jeans, baby pink hoodie and matching bow. Samantha had promised that if she was a good girl, then she would be allowed to wear her new sneakers and maybe the jacket, and that was the only reason why Nelly was trying so hard not to pout.

"Hello Amanda," Samantha greeted from the door as Amanda walked inside. Samantha took her coat and bag and hung them on one of the wall hooks before inviting her through to the living room.

"Hey cutie," Amanda said, standing behind Nelly, who bent her head back and looked up at her.

"Hi Amanda," Nelly said before going back to her art. Amanda smiled and looked around the apartment.

"Did you move in with her, Sammy?" Amanda asked as Samantha handed her a drink.

"No, we moved into it together," Nelly called from the living room, making Samantha smirk.

"She's very independent and didn't want me to just put her up in the penthouse," Samantha explained as they walked back into the living room and sat on the couch. The fireplace warmed the space, and the crackling of the fire mixed with the taste of whiskey felt peaceful.

"It's actually really lovely," Amanda said approvingly, unbeknownst to her easing Samantha's fears.

"What are you making there, Nelly?" Amanda asked, leaning forward and eyeing Nelly expecting a response.

"It's a tiger," Nelly replied, looking back at

Samantha, wanting approval.

"It's very good," Amanda added, seeing the detail and care Nelly had taken. Nelly continued to work on her artwork before Samantha leaned down and pulled her up onto the couch and into her arms.

"What do we say when someone gives us a compliment, baby girl?" Samantha asked as Nelly leaned her body into Samantha's but turned her head to face Amanda.

"Thank you," Nelly softly said before burying her face into Samantha's cleavage and sucking her thumb.

"She's feeling a little bit, little tonight," Samantha explained as Amanda watched somewhat longingly.

"Oh, I can see that," Amanda replied, reaching out and stroking Nelly's back affectionately.

"I need to finish getting ready, would you mind watching her for a moment," Samantha said as she kissed Nelly's forehead and placed her back on the floor.

"Not at all," Amanda said, the eagerness in her voice evident. Samantha winked at Nelly, who smirked back at her as she disappeared into their bedroom.

"Want to play a game?" Nelly asked, walking over to where she and Samantha kept a deck of cards.

"Like, poker?" Amanda teased, making Nelly laugh.

"I was thinking more like, snap," Nelly said, taking out the cards and passing them to Amanda. She shuffled them, dealt them out, and as they began to play, Amanda snapped the cards, Nelly's hand on top of hers a fraction too slow.

"You'll have to do better than that, baby girl," Amanda laughed as she took the cards, and they began to play once more. Samantha could hear the laughter coming from the living room as she finished her makeup and sprayed perfume. She and Nelly had decided that they would let Amanda in on the non-sexual side of the dynamic for the evening, and by all accounts, it seemed to be going well. She turned her head and looked out onto the scene, which played out in front of her and smiled, just as she heard Amanda's hand come down hard on Nelly's.

"Ouch!" Nelly squealed, Amanda's eyes going wide as she realized that she had brought her hand down far too hard on top of Nelly's.

"Oh, sweetie, I'm sorry, are you ok?" Amanda said as Nelly frowned and pouted, trying to be ok.

"You've got to be tough if you want to play with the big girls, honey," Samantha said, walking out and going to the fridge to get an icepack.

"I am tough," Nelly said, slightly insulted. Samantha walked over to where Nelly was sitting and picked her up. She sat her on her lap and rocked her gently as she wrapped the icepack around her hand. Amanda got up and poured herself and Samantha another drink before joining them on the couch.

"Maybe we should have stuck with

coloring," Amanda said, surprised when Nelly reached for her. She looked at Samantha, who smiled kindly at her as she took Nelly in her arms and wrapped them around her. Amanda smelt like jasmine and something else that Nelly couldn't figure out, and she snuggled into the nook of Amanda's neck.

"Oh, I could just hold you forever," Amanda said as she melted into Nelly, Samantha reaching out and stroking Nelly's cheek.

"She is a sweetheart. That's for sure," Samantha replied, taking Nelly's paci and placing it in her mouth as she closed her eyes and relaxed into Amanda's embrace.

"We are going to be late for our reservation if we stay here, though," Samantha added, Nelly opening her eyes as her tummy rumbled.

"And I think, little miss, needs something to eat and soon!" Amanda laughed, rubbing Nelly's tummy before she could stop herself.

"But first," Nelly said, ripping her bow headband from her hair and messing her hair up so that it had that flowy effect she liked so much. Samantha laughed and got up to get her sneakers and jacket.

"I told her that she had to wear it before we left the house because she just looks so divine in it," Samantha explained, passing Nelly her things.

Nelly held both Samantha's and Amanda's hand on the way to the restaurant, only letting go once they walked inside.

"See, Mommy wasn't going to let you look out of place," Samantha whispered to Nelly as they sat down. Nelly held Samantha's hand under the table and squeezed it gently. It had been fun so far, and Nelly liked that Amanda never tried to overstep.

As the night went on, Samantha could see that Amanda had taken a shine to Nelly, but in true Nelly style, once she knew that Amanda liked her, she had begun to pull away. Amanda had decided to let any thoughts she had of further play go and turned her attention to the waitress, causing

Samantha and Nelly to laugh at the obvious flirting which occurred between the two of them. After dinner, Amanda excused her self and went outside, explaining that she needed to take the phone call, which had interrupted their evening. Samantha and Nelly turned toward each other and began talking while they waited for Amanda to return.

"Hey, yeah, I am here with both of them," Amanda said down the phone.

"No, I can tell you for certain that they don't have any idea," she added, answering the person on the other end of the line.

"Well, they don't live there anymore. So it won't be that difficult," Amanda said.

"Good," said Wendy, on the other line.

"What do you want me to do then?" Amanda replied. Wendy had stalked Samantha online after she convinced herself that Samantha had been the reason she couldn't get Nelly back. She had found Amanda in Samantha's friends' list and contacted her after learning that she had a large amount of gambling debt. Wendy had resolved herself to the plan that if she couldn't have Nelly, that she was going to take her for everything that she and Samantha had, and was going to rob them. Amanda had agreed to help her after Wendy had promised to clear the debt and that no harm would come to either Samantha and Nelly. Amanda knew that Samantha was wealthy and assumed that she would simply go out and buy everything new.

"All you have to do is send me their address, and keep them out for the next two hours," Wendy hissed down the phone.

"Fine," Amanda replied, ending the phone call and sending her their address. She inhaled sharply before nodding her head as she thought about where they could all go for the next two hours.

Chapter 11

"All good?" Samantha asked as Amanda sat back down. Nelly had gone to get the dessert menus.

"Yeah. Hey, why don't we do something a little unexpected and take Nelly to the movies tonight?" Amanda suggested, hoping that Samantha would agree to the idea.

"I don't know. It's already pretty late," Samantha replied, looking at the time on her phone.

"But I don't know when I will see you again. Come on, my treat," Amanda pressed just as Nelly sat back down.

"I like treats," she said, looking up at Samantha.

"Amanda wants to take you to the movies," Samantha said, smiling at the joy in Nelly's eyes as she looked from Amanda to Samantha.

"So, is it a yes from your Mommy then?" Amanda teased, looking at Samantha, who just rolled her eyes.

"Yeah. Let's skip dessert here and get treats when we are at the cinema," she said, paying for dinner before getting up. Nelly looked online for movie options as they walked the four blocks to the cinema, deciding on a thriller which surprised Samantha.

"You are going to be so scared I can just see you all over me while I'm trying to watch it," she said, taking her phone from Nelly's hands.

"Well, if you don't want to cuddle her, I certainly will," Amanda teased, running her fingers through Nelly's hair.

They arrived at the cinema, ordered their tickets and snacks, and went inside. There was only one other couple that sat in the middle of the audience, so Samantha directed Nelly and Amanda to some seats in the back.

"This is so exciting," Nelly said, clapping her hands.

"Shh," came a whisper from both Samantha and Amanda, only making Nelly laugh. They sat down, Nelly in the middle, and it didn't take more than ten minutes before Nelly was snuggling into Samantha's side, the suspense almost too much for her to handle.

"It's ok, baby girl. Mommy has got you, this is all just make-believe," Samantha lovingly whispered as she put up the armrest so that Nelly could be even closer to her. Amanda sneakily looked at the time. Right now, she knew that Wendy would be in their apartment, watching as furniture was loaded into the removalist truck. She thought about the debt that she would be free from and tried to rid herself of the guilt of doing this to her friend.

It's just money, and Sammy has heaps of it, Amanda told herself for the hundredth time as the movie reached its climax. Nelly jumped and burried her face into Samantha's side, Samantha wrapping her arm around the girl and patting her affectionately for the rest of the film.

"So I might have made a mistake," Nelly giggled as they walked home. Nelly refused to let go of Samantha's hand and held on firmly whenever they passed something which reminded her of the movie they had just seen.

"You're quiet," Samantha said to Amanda. Amanda just smiled at her.

"I am more tired than I thought I would be," she lied. The truth was that she was being eaten up inside by the betrayal she had done to her friend. They said goodnight, Amanda holding onto Samantha for a longer time than necessary before going their separate ways.

"Until the next, ten years or so," Samantha called as they walked away, causing Amanda to laugh and wave back at her before turning around and phoning Wendy.

"They are on their way home now, if you aren't already gone, you need to go now," Amanda said, the knot in her stomach becoming physically painful.

"Good job. I got everything I wanted. The money is in your account. Don't contact me again," Wendy replied, hanging up the phone and driving out of Samantha's and Nelly's street just as she saw them turn the corner. Amanda sighed and checked her account. Sure enough, Wendy had stayed true to her word and put a little extra on top for her troubles. Amanda rolled her eyes, surprised in herself that she could be so easily manipulated.

"What the fuck," Samantha said as she opened their apartment door. She walked in slowly, taking out her pistol from her purse. She heard Holly and Sasha barking from the courtyard and frowned at what she was seeing.

"Jesus, Samantha," Nelly said as she saw Samantha draw her gun, finally understanding why once she too walked inside.

"Baby. Stay behind me," Samantha said as she slowly walked around the apartment. The place was bare. Nothing was messed up, nothing was broken, but it was bare—the paintings on the walls, the furniture, the rugs were all gone. The crockery and cutlery were all still in the kitchen, but the alcohol had been stripped from the bar. Samantha walked into their bedroom and saw that the bed was gone, along with all of their clothes, sports gear, jewelry, and shoes. Their perfumes, hair products, and technical gear was also gone, and Nelly cried when she saw that her bunny, which she slept with, was also missing.

"Mommy," Nelly said as she looked up at Samantha with tears running down her face.

"It's going to be alright, baby girl. Mommy is going to make this alright," Samantha said as she put her gun away, deeming that there was no threat, that there was nothing at all.

"What are we going to do?" Nelly asked as they sat on the floor in the middle of the living room. Samantha was grateful they had left the fridge, as she took a can of coke out for herself and Nelly.

"We just have to buy it all again, honey.

Which is going to be fun, I mean, you are always saying you want to go on a shopping spree," Samantha replied, trying to find the positive in the situation.

"We will have to do something with the dogs. Maybe Val from next door can look after them for a week or so," Samantha suggested, Nelly, nodding her head in agreement.

"Where will we sleep?" Nelly asked, crawling into Samantha's lap.

"We will go to a hotel tonight, maybe for the next few weeks, depending on how long the bed takes to arrive. I'm going to call in sick for the rest of the week. I think you should too. If you tell them what has happened, I think they will be understanding," Samantha said as she got up and took Nelly's hand in hers.

"Thanks, Mommy," Nelly said, causing Samantha to look down at her in confusion.

"For looking after me," Nelly explained, making Samantha laugh.

"I don't think I've done a very good job at

looking after you, baby girl. Look at the mess we are in right now. I've never been robbed in my life! I feel like I've failed you," Samantha said before she unlocked the courtyard and put the dogs on their leads. Samantha shook her head in disbelief before grabbing her phone and walking out the door.

Val had agreed to look after the dogs saying that she would love the company and before they knew it, Samantha and Nelly were walking down the street and towards a five-star hotel.

"You haven't, though, Mommy. Maybe we should reconsider moving into a more, safer neighborhood after all, though," Nelly said, feeling as though it was her fault because she had been the one who had wanted to make sure she could pay for half the rent. Samantha had said she could just move in with her, but Nelly was too independent just to be kept, she wanted Samantha to know she could hold her own.

"How about we just agree that this sucks, that it is neither of our faults and while we are looking for a completely new interior, we also look for a new apartment?" Samantha suggested as they neared a hotel.

"Agreed," Nelly replied, hoping that she could go to sleep at last.

Chapter 12

Samantha and Nelly opened the door to their hotel room, turned off the lights, and fell into bed, not waking until mid-morning.

"Hey, sweetie," Samantha said as Nelly pulled a face.

"Yeah, I think a shower and teeth clean is in order as well," Samantha laughed as they both got up.

"I still can't believe it. I think we should get some clothes first because we only have what we wore last night," Nelly said as she stripped and got into the shower. Turning the water on and washing her hair and body as Samantha watched. It was going to be their first-year anniversary in three weeks, and she had planned to take Nelly to Paris, something which would definitely have to wait.

"I think we should just get the basics of

everything first. I don't want it to take too long to get stuff. We need to get back on our feet," Samantha said, undressing and pushing Nelly against the wall.

"You missed a spot," Samantha seductively said as she rubbed between Nelly's thighs and over her pussy.

"No, that's always the first place I do," Nelly replied, winking at Samantha, who laughed. Nelly wrapped her arms around Samantha's shoulders as she was finger fucked, moaning into Samantha's shoulder as she was brought close to an orgasm.

"That's enough," Samantha suddenly said, pulling out of Nelly, who whined, wanting release.

"That is so mean!" Nelly said, spanking Samantha's ass, gaining her attention once more.

"Don't hit Mommy," Samantha said, clear warning in her tone, which Nelly thought about if she wanted to listen to or ignore. Deciding it was best to listen, Nelly got out of the shower and back into her clothes. Samantha soon joined her, and they wrote a list of all the clothes they would need to buy.

"Mommy. I can't afford to get all this stuff. And I know you'll say that you can buy it for me, but I feel bad about you getting it. Especially since I know your version of basic and mine are very different," Nelly said as they walked down the street.

"Honey. It's Mommy's job to look after you. You don't need to feel bad about that. If it makes you feel better, you can tell me what stores you want us to go into? I know you like a few second-hand stores, and I'm happy to get you something there. I just want to make sure you have everything you need, alright?" Samantha said as they walked into a big department store. Samantha took Nelly to the lingerie section first, and Nelly walked around and found different things she liked, and it didn't take her very long to have a full selection. Samantha, on the other hand, took so long as she wanted to try everything on that she had told Nelly to take a copy of the list and go around the store to try and find other things she needed. What she didn't tell Nelly was that she was going to use that time to arrange a few things. The first being a new place to live.

She rang her cousin, who owned the company she first rented the penthouse from and asked him if there was any property that would be fitting. Delighting in the fact that he said there was a newly built apartment in the heart of the city that had river and park views. Wasting no time at all once he had sent her the photos, she told him to fill her out an application and send it to them.

The benefits of family, she thought to herself as she exited the change room.

"Oh, hey, I found like most things on this list," Nelly said as she walked over to Samantha, who put the pieces she had just tried on, on the counter.

"Can you ring these up with whatever she's getting, please," Samantha kindly said before leading Nelly away.

"What do you think of this?" Samantha

asked as she showed Nelly the photos making her sigh.

"I'm just going to have to get used to you looking after me, aren't I?" Nelly asked, causing Samantha's pussy to tingle at her final surrender.

"Yes, you are, sweetie. And about time too," Samantha replied, kissing Nelly on the top of her head.

"It's really beautiful, I'm not going to ask how you manage to afford it," Nelly said as she walked into the winter coat section.

"Good girl," Samantha answered, patting Nelly's ass affectionately before disappearing into another section of the store.

They emerged hours later after having lunch and had their purchases sent to the hotel. Nelly was exhausted and had become somewhat bratty as she and Samantha rested in the hotel room.

"Mommy wants a rest, baby girl," Samantha said when she took the television remote off Nelly and turned the tv off.

"But Mommy," Nelly whined as she coped a look from Samantha.

"Oh, you'd better not," Samantha warned. Nelly just huffed, rolled her eyes, and crossed her arms.

"I don't think I'm the only one who needs a nap," Samantha said, taking off her clothes and walking over to Nelly in her lingerie.

"I don't need a nap," Nelly huffed, annoyed that she only moments before yawned.

"Oh, I see," Samantha replied, making Nelly more annoyed that she wasn't taking the bait.

"Well, come here anyway, miss I don't need a nap," Samantha said, pulling Nelly to her nipple and spanking her ass hard when she tried to refuse.

"Don't be a bad girl for Mommy, baby," Samantha calmly said as she continued to spank Nelly until she stopped fussing and began to suckle.

"Good girl," Samantha cooed, cracking her neck from side to side and pulling her hair to one side. Nelly frowned as she obeyed Samantha, making Samantha laugh and begin to rub over Nelly's jeans.

"I think these need to come off," Samantha said, unzipping Nelly's jeans and helping her wriggle out of them. Nelly continued to nurse as Samantha slipped her hand in Nelly's panties and stroked her softly.

"Such a good girl for Mommy," Samantha said, gently beginning to finger fuck Nelly who moaned against the thick nipple in her mouth.

"Mommy," Nelly slowly moaned.

"I shouldn't hear little girls who have Mommy's nipple in their mouths," Samantha said, repositioning her nipple in Nelly's mouth. Samantha continued to take her, stroking her g-spot as Nelly wriggled in her arms, desperate to be allowed to orgasm. Samantha held Nelly's mouth to her breast as she filled her with a third finger, stretching Nelly's pussy and making her cry out in pleasure and pain.

"Breath through it, honey. You're safe with

Mommy," Samantha lovingly whispered as she took the girl as her heart desired. Nelly tried to pull back as the orgasm flooded her senses, but her body fell limp in Samantha's arms, her nipple being lazily played within Nelly's mouth.

"Mommy," Nelly said as Samantha took her off one breast just to put her on the second.

"Are you still going to try and tell Mommy lies about you not needing a nap?" Samantha asked, fully aware that Nelly always needed a nap after sex. Nelly just slowly shook her head and closed her eyes as Samantha squeezed milk into her mouth, forcing her to continue to suckle.

"I'm not finished with you yet," Samantha said as she reached into her handbag and took out the new strapon she had bought without Nelly seeing. Lying Nelly on the bed, Samantha secured the belt to her hips and stroked the dildo predatorily as she looked at Nelly's tired body on the bed.

"You are so perfect," Samantha said as she grabbed Nelly's ankles and pulled her towards the tip of the dildo. Samantha rubbed it with lube before moving behind Nelly and pushing the tip into Nelly's pussy, making her put her ass up much to Samantha's delight.

"Good girl, you'll take this fucking like Mommy's little slut, won't you baby girl?" Samantha said as she slowly pushed herself inside of Nelly's wet pussy. Moaning, Samantha held her hips in position as she completely buried her dildo inside of Nelly, who gasped at how filled she was.

"You know how to make it stop," Samantha said before she began to take Nelly from behind rhythmically. Nelly bit her bottom lip and twerked for Samantha as she was fucked, making Samantha reach around and rub her clit. The weight of Samantha's breasts on her back made Nelly moan as she felt herself enveloped by the older woman as she aggressively fucked her.

"That's it," Samantha said in a low, aroused voice as she felt Nelly's pussy juices squirt out around the dildo and onto her thighs. With a few final thrusts, Samantha pulled out of Nelly and watched as she collapsed in a heap on the bed. Bringing her knees to her chest, Nelly breathed through the after the shock of the multiple orgasms Samantha had just given her. Samantha took the strapon off and walked into the bathroom, cursing her period from stopping Nelly from fucking her as well.

"Here, baby," Samantha said as she walked back to where Nelly was still lying. She scooped Nelly up in her arms, and carried her to the shower, washed her down, and then took her to the other bed in the hotel suite.

"Mommy got you something special, little one," Samantha said, taking out a light pink onesie and gently dressing Nelly, happy that she didn't have to fight her.

"There, Mommy's perfect little girl," Samantha cooed as Nelly snuggled into her side and began to fall asleep.

Chapter 13

"Mommy?" Nelly softly said as she woke up a few hours later. Samantha had rested as well but had also spent a considerable amount of time online looking at and buying furniture for the next apartment.

"Just out here, baby girl," Samantha called out from the balcony. Nelly walked to the door and looked at Samantha.

"You look like you are in your element, Mommy," Nelly said, observing the bottle of champagne and room service that Samantha had set up.

"Well, Mommy never likes to work on an empty stomach," Samantha replied, laughing.

"Come here and sit on my lap," she quickly added as she saw Nelly begin to walk away. Nelly turned back around and made her way outside, resting her head on Samantha's shoulder as she looked on the new laptop screen at the luxurious furniture collection displayed.

"Have you left anything for me to decide on, Mommy?" Nelly asked as Samantha showed her all the items she had purchased.

"Of course. You are going to pick out the most important elements, the decorations," Samantha said, making Nelly laugh.

"Thank goodness!" She teased and began to scroll through sites looking for bath towels and bedding.

"Mommy," Nelly whined as she felt Samantha's fingers begin to open the bottom of her onesie.

"Shh," Samantha replied as she groped Nelly, pushing her forward so her elbows were on the glass table and her back curved in.

"You look so sexy," Samantha whispered as Nelly felt her move the strap on in her pants.

"Are you packing?" Nelly laughed, turning her head to face Samantha just to have Samantha grab her messy ponytail and direct her head to face forward.

"Yep," Samantha replied as she pulled it from her pants and positioned Nelly over the top.

"Sit," Samantha commanded, hearing Nelly gasp and moan as she sat on Samantha's lap, her dildo entering her slowly. But Samantha wasn't interested in waiting and bucked her hips up, filling Nelly and guided her back down so that she was secured on top of her.

"Mommy, it's too big," Nelly moaned, feeling Samantha begin to bounce her on her lap.

"No, it's not," Samantha replied, reaching around to rub Nelly's clit, feeling her take it more easily as she was stimulated.

"See?" Samantha said smugly as Nelly curved her back even more in an attempt to have the tip hit her g-spot.

"Bounce for Mommy," Samantha commanded and held onto Nelly's hips, enjoying the feeling of her ass grinding down on her lap.

"Mommy, no," Nelly said as Samantha placed her thumb in Nelly's mouth, pulling her body back and fucking her less deeply.

"Don't say no to Mommy, kitten," Samantha plainly said as she denied Nelly an orgasm. Samantha could feel Nelly begin to give in, which always made her body come from the slightest of touches, so she held her in place, getting turned on by Nelly's futile attempts to maintain stimulation and pulled out of the girl.

"Get on your knees," Samantha said as she moved forward on the chair. Nelly obeyed and opened her mouth, knowing what Samantha wanted.

"Good girl," she cooed as she slid down Nelly's throat until her eyes watered. Keeping herself inside her mouth, Samantha stroked Nelly's head lovingly.

"Swallow," Samantha commanded, ramming Nelly's throat when she took too long.

"Don't make Mommy wait," Samantha warned before slowly face fucking Nelly. Samantha knew that Nelly's knees would hurt, but as she stood up and continued to force her dildo down

Nelly's throat, the sight turned her on too much. She began to rub her clit and pinch her nipples, her head rolling back as her hips pounded into Nelly's mouth.

Just one, Samantha thought to herself as she felt her orgasm building.

"Put your arms behind your back and look up at me," Samantha instructed, moaning as Nelly followed her orders and looked beautifully submissive.

"Yes," Samantha slowly moaned as she felt her pussy flood and finally took her dildo from Nelly's lips. Nelly put her hands on her thighs and waited patiently, her knees sore and red.

"Thank you, baby girl," Samantha said, reaching out and lifting Nelly up, catching her when her legs gave way.

"Mommy's got you. I'm not going to let anything bad happen to you," Samantha said as she led Nelly inside. She took off the strapon and looked through the shopping bags for some cream, finding it and also finding a magazine for Nelly.

"Here, sugar," Samantha said as she passed Nelly the magazine before rubbing her knees with the soothing cream.

"Does that feel nice?" Samantha said Nelly's cheeky sparkle in her eye, telling her that she was feeling better already.

"No," Nelly said plainly.

"No?" Questioned Samantha playfully, looking at Nelly shake her head. Samantha put the cream away and went to sit beside Nelly on the bed.

"What do you need then, sweetie," Samantha asked, sweeping Nelly's hair from her face.

"I need a cookie," Nelly replied in her little voice, making Samantha laugh.

"A cookie?" She questioned, eyeing her playfully.

"And a chocolate shake?" Samantha added, making Nelly's eyes go wide with excitement.

"Yes, please, Mommy!" Nelly replied quickly.

"Come on then. We better drop into Val's and check on the dogs while we are out," Samantha suggested as they began to get ready to leave.

Chapter 14

It was five days before Samantha and Nelly were able to move into their new apartment. Samantha had organized the furniture delivery people to turn up to the new house and unpack everything and another company to place it beautifully in the house. She had taken Nelly down to the park with the dogs, and they had spent the whole day out while their once empty apartment was transformed into the grand vision they had designed together.

"I hope that is the last adventure we have for a while," Nelly said as they walked the dogs up the street and around the corner to a 24-hour diner. Samantha tied the dogs to the table leg, and Nelly went inside and took two menus before returning outside and sitting down.

"I think it will be. I'm sure that Amanda had something to do with it. It was just too much of a coincidence," Samantha said, looking over the menu and picking out blueberry pancakes. They watched as the sun went down and the stars came out, Samantha getting a phone call to say that the apartment was ready.

"Wonderful, thank you," came her reply. Nelly had gotten used to Samantha taking care of things, and she sipped her coffee as Samantha finished the conversation. She thought back to when they had first met and smiled to herself, half proud that she had been somebody that someone like Samantha would be interested in. Nelly was a different woman than the girl who Samantha had first met, and she wondered how long her youthful looks would last before Samantha wanted to find somebody new and younger and more, princess, in distress like.

"Ready to go?" Samantha said, interrupting Nelly's thoughts.

"What? Yeah, sorry I was just thinking," Nelly said, getting up and taking Sasha's lead in her hand.

"You know, we have our anniversary coming up. I was thinking it might be nice to do something for it," Nelly said as they walked to their new home. Samantha wrapped her arm around Nelly and looked down at her and smiled.

"I was thinking the same. But maybe we could do something locally? I think having some calm after this storm might be in order," Samantha replied, Nelly, nodding in agreement.

"So, maybe we could stay in town and go to the ABDL convention that weekend?" Nelly suggested, hoping that Samantha would agree. Nelly had seen an advertisement in one of the online communities she was a member of and had been eager to go.

"Really?" Samantha said, imagining seeing countless babies and all sorts of stuff she wasn't interested in.

"Please, Mommy," Nelly begged, turning to walk backward but facing Samantha.

"We might find something new or cool or something," Nelly said, Samantha, smiling at her lovingly as she led her out of the way of oncoming people.

"We don't have to go for the whole time, but just like, a day or so and see what's there," Nelly continued, stopping at the corner and waiting for the traffic to slow.

"Alright. But we are going to go to that new restaurant, the one that serves lobster as well," Samantha said, making Nelly laugh.

"That's hardly a hard compromise to make," Nelly smirked.

Samantha held Nelly's hand as they walked into their new home, and they both sighed in happiness, looking around the space.

"You did alright, Mommy," Nelly said, playfully nudging Samantha. Nelly's eyes sparkled as she looked at the home, which looked like it came from the pages of a luxury home magazine.

"Yes, I did," Samantha said, feeling rather impressed with herself.

"This will do nicely. You know, maybe

having our stuff stolen turned out to be the best thing for us," Samantha said, confusing Nelly.

"How do you mean?" Nelly asked as Samantha led her into one of the spare rooms.

"Mommy," Nelly whispered in surprise as Samantha pushed her into a room that had been set up as a room just for her. Nelly looked at Samantha in disbelief.

"Surprise, baby girl," Samantha said as she sat down on the day bed that was set up against the wall.

"How did you organize this without me knowing?!" Nelly exclaimed as she looked over her new things. There was a skateboard rack with three boards already lying in the spaces and a bookshelf with fashion books as well as a craft table by the window. There was a shelf with a selection of fluffy bunnies from her favorite brand and a new laptop on a wooden desk.

"Well, you sleep a lot, honey. So I just did everything when you were snuggled up next to me," Samantha said as Nelly opened the cupboard and saw the collection of house clothes and onesies.

"Mommy," Nelly said, tilting her head and rolling her eyes.

"What? Don't even pretend that you don't need your paci sometimes," Samantha said as she rubbed her nipples.

"But not tonight?" Nelly asked knowingly, coming over to Samantha, who wrapped her arms around her and held her tight.

"No, not tonight," Samantha agreed, rubbing her breasts against Nelly and kissing her on the top of her head and enjoying how the girl felt in her arms.

"But first, let's try out that new bath, little one," Samantha said, gently standing up and pushing Nelly backward.

"Can we use the spa features, please, Mommy?" Nelly asked, but Samantha was already shaking her head no.

"Not tonight. I want to get clean and get into bed. Mommy is tired, baby girl," Samantha explained, happy that Nelly accepted her answer and didn't push the issue.

"You can have your bath toys though, honey," Samantha suggested as they entered the huge room, and Nelly stripped, telling the house to play music and dancing around the bathroom for Samantha.

"Easy, little girl," Samantha said as Nelly slipped off her t-shirt, and Samantha caught her in her arms.

"Thanks, Mommy," Nelly giggle as she got into the bath and began to splash around happily.

"You're little tonight," Samantha said as she got in behind Nelly, delighted that they both fit very comfortably. Samantha washed Nelly's body, lathering her up in body wash and rinsing her off gently as Nelly played with the soapsuds. Samantha bathed herself quickly before getting out of the bath and leaving Nelly to play while she dried herself and got into her short pajama shorts and matching singlet. Nelly loved it when Samantha wore this type of thing to bed because it hugged her curves, and she could also see her nipples poking through the material.

"Out you come, little girl," Samantha said as she took Nelly's hands and helped her stand up. Nelly shivered as the cold night air hit her body, and Samantha wrapped her in a thick fluffy pink towel to dry her off.

"I think you'd better go to your room, baby girl. Mommy is going to diaper you tonight," Samantha said as Nelly quietly and sleepily walked into her room and lay on the floor. Samantha took a diaper down from the box on top of the cupboard as well as some powder and began to diaper Nelly, who quietly sucked on the corner of the towel.

"See, I knew you'd need Mommy tonight," Samantha said as Nelly reached up to grab on Samantha's big breasts with hung in front of Nelly. Samantha chose a black onesie with pink thigh high socks and helped Nelly to her feet, just for her to drop back down to her knees and lift up her arms.

"Oh, Mommy's little one," Samantha cooed

as she bent down to pick Nelly up and carried her into their bedroom. Tucking Nelly in, Samantha lay next to her and watched as Nelly began to suckle from her without any instruction.

"Mommy's special girl," Samantha said as she closed her eyes and let Nelly have all of her.

Chapter 15

"I know you couldn't think of nothing worse, but I am really happy we are going to this," Nelly said in the car on the way to the ABDL convention two weeks later. It was true, Samantha could think of many more places she would like to go to rather than this, but it was important to Nelly, and she could hardly say no to the girl.

"It's not that I hate the idea, I just only like you. So I don't care what all these other people do," Samantha replied. Truth be told, she was worried that other Mommies wouldn't think she was a very good one, or that Nelly wasn't a real little or middle because she didn't subscribe to many of the stereotypical elements of the kink. But she wasn't about to let Nelly know of her fears when she knew they were just silly insecurities.

"We are here," Samantha said, trying to sound enthused. Nelly looked at all the people and bit her bottom lip.

"Maybe this was a bad idea," she said, looking at Samantha. Samantha frowned and looked at Nelly, wondering why she would think that.

"Like, I don't really have that whole vibe going, you know?" Nelly said, making Samantha laugh.

"I might feel the same way about myself. Let's just go in and have a look around, and if it's not for us, then we can leave, and if there's something you want to look at, then we can stay, alright. No pressure, honey," Samantha said, unbuckling Nelly's seat belt.

"Thanks, Mommy," Nelly said, getting out of the car.

"Maybe I can call you Mommy in here without people wondering what the deal is?" Nelly asked as they walked into the convention and stopped in their tracks. They looked at each other and smirked, knowing that they would probably stay for longer than they had initially thought.

"Yeah, I have a feeling you can," Samantha said as a man dressed in full ADBL attire casually walked passed them.

They spent time strolling through the differing setups. There were cartoonists and stuffed toy displays and paci's that could be personally designed and decorated. Samantha took her blazer off and held it over her shoulder as they walked from vendor to vendor, Nelly's eyes and subtle smile, telling Samantha more than her words. Samantha ran her hand through her hair, closing her eyes and shaking her head as Nelly turned to look at her, captivated. Samantha opened her eyes to find more than just Nelly's eyes on her, and it made her smirk that she could still catch the gaze of strangers. Nelly didn't miss a beat either, and walked back over to Samantha, took her hand and walked with her towards the next display.

"Oh, is somebody jealous?" Samantha teased, causing Nelly to roll her eyes.

"As if," said Nelly, far too defensively to fool Samantha, who just laughed and twirled her as they walked.

"What time was that event you wanted to go to, baby?" Samantha asked as she saw a large group of people making their way to the entrance of the convention.

"Oh yeah. I was going to go with some people to make a stuffie," Nelly said, pulling out her phone to check the time as Samantha checked her watch.

"Oh. I got a message. I think that's them," Nelly said, tilting her head to the group, following as she replied to the message. Samantha thought it was adorable that Nelly was nervous and shy as she approached the group.

"Hey, are you guys heading off to make stuffies, or am I in the wrong place?" Nelly said, surprised that she was feeling so confident and shy at the same time.

"Hey, yeah, that's us. I'm Joshy," a man said, waving at Nelly, making her smile and look back at Samantha.

"I'm Nelly," Nelly said, shrugging her

shoulder and letting her hair fall around her face as she felt Samantha come up behind her.

"See you later, baby," she said, kissing Nelly's cheek and putting her headband in her hair before winking at her and walking back into the convention, she had seen some stickers that she knew Nelly would love and wanted to buy her a few things before she got back.

Bye, Mommy, Nelly text as she walked down the street with the new group of people.

Were you too shy to say that in front of your new friends? Samantha replied, knowing that it would make Nelly blush.

Maybe, Nelly replied, making Samantha laugh as she looked at the different emojis Nelly had added to the end of her message. Samantha just smirked as she put her phone away and went to the various vendor stalls. She knew that she spoilt Nelly, some other Mommies had told her so on the online community she was a member of, but she didn't care. She liked that she was in a position to spoil her baby, and Nelly was such a great partner in all aspects of their relationship that Samantha didn't mind treating her to special things when she saw them. Although Nelly leaned more to a middle, she still loved stickers and wearing a diaper sometimes, so Samantha bought her a pack of diapers with cute animal faces peeking out as well as a matching snapback of a husky puppy.

She is going to look so cute in this, Samantha excitedly thought as she paid the vendor before looking around the rest of the convention.

Nelly ended up making a pastel fuzzy bunny, which Samantha laughed at the moment she saw it.

"Baby girl, what on earth is that?" She asked, making Nelly laugh in shock.

"It is my bunny," Nelly giggled as she was wrapped up in Samantha's arms. Samantha kissed the top of Nelly's head and felt Nelly snuggle into her.

"Come on, little one. Let's go back home,"

Samantha said as Nelly followed her to the car. Samantha was happy that they lived in the same city as the convention as she drove down the street, seeing how busy the hotels were. People were everywhere, and just the general bustling atmosphere of the city made her wonder how hard it would be for Nelly to get to sleep that night.

"Baby?" Samantha asked, placing her hand on Nelly's thigh and turning her head to look at her. Smiling, Samantha saw Nelly cuddling her new stuffie and thought it best to continue to let her sleep.

Turns out, it won't be very hard at all, Samantha thought to herself as she felt Nelly turn and cuddle onto Samantha's arm, which was still in Nelly's lap.

"Shh, we are nearly home, princess," Samantha said as she continued to drive her happy, sleepy baby girl home.

Who is Tina Moore?

Tina Moore has enjoyed the lifestyle of a Mommy Domme for several years. She began secretly exploring kink and BDSM in her youth and found her love of being a strict Mommy Domme in early 2000. Tina Moore slowly became more comfortable and confident through making friends in the community and exploring the lifestyle and now openly celebrates being a Mommy Domme to her little.

Before becoming an author, Tina Moore worked in the finance sector, but it was through the encouragement of her current little that she took the leap and wrote her first MDLG book, Nancy's Little One.

From then on, Tina Moore continued to combine her experiences and desires, as well as the sweet and naughty things her baby girl does, to bring you tantalizing and salacious stories about both MDLG and DDLG relationships and the ABDL littles and middles who enjoy them.

Follow her on:

Author Page on Amazon

Instagram @tinamoore.kdp